"No More Pretending. It's Just You and Me."

Megan knew that now was the time to stop. With no imaginary characters to hide behind, she'd be wearing her heart on her sleeve, and she was afraid of her feelings. She knew all this. But her lips parted under the hungry probe of his tongue and her arms wound around him. As control slipped away, she fought off the drowning waves of pleasure with a cold splash of reality. There was a tomorrow and a next day.

Abruptly she pushed away from him. "No, Colt." It was a hoarse whisper. "Don't complicate things."

MELODIE ADAMS
has been strongly influenced in her writing by her parents. "Their insatiable desire to live life to the fullest was definite insurance against a dull childhood." Melodie and her husband Steve love to travel, and have seen everything from the Bitterroot Mountain Range in Montana to the Florida Gulf Coast—and a lot of places in between.

Dear Reader:

I'd like to take this opportunity to thank you for all your support and encouragement of Silhouette Romances.

Many of you write in regularly, telling us what you like best about Silhouette, which authors are your favorites. This is a tremendous help to us as we strive to publish the best contemporary romances possible.

All the romances from Silhouette Books are for you, so enjoy this book and the many stories to come.

Karen Solem
Editor-in-Chief
Silhouette Books

MELODIE ADAMS
I'll Fly the Flags

Silhouette Romance

Published by Silhouette Books New York
America's Publisher of Contemporary Romance

SILHOUETTE BOOKS, a Division of Simon & Schuster, Inc.
1230 Avenue of the Americas, New York, N.Y. 10020

ISBN: 0-671-57265-2

First Silhouette Books printing December, 1983

10 9 8 7 6 5 4 3 2 1

Map by Ray Lundgren

America's Publisher of Contemporary Romance

Printed in the U.S.A.

BC91

For Bill,

There isn't enough space on a page to express my gratitude, so I dedicate this story to you, the man who inspired it.

It is only a small token of appreciation for your time, your help, your encouragement and your interest—those things you have so generously used to mold what I thought could only be a dream into a reality.

This is for you, Bill, for everything you are and everything you've done. Thank you.

Melodie Adams

NORTHERN ONTARIO

HUDSON BAY

JAMES BAY

ONTARIO

QUEBEC

RAINY LAKE

MINNESOTA

LAKE SUPERIOR

MICHIGAN

WISCONSIN

MICHIGAN

Chapter One

The reflection in the glass door was markedly different from the usual traffic that passed through the entrance.

Caramel-brown hair with a dominant gold sheen curled softly under on the ends, splayed thick and rich across the shoulders of a khaki bush jacket. Belted at a slim waist and left partially unbuttoned, the jacket allowed a glimpse of the silky red blouse beneath. Smooth designer jeans were tucked into the tops of high-heeled leather fashion boots. The blue denim material did more to emphasize than conceal long, shapely legs.

Oblivious to her mirrored image, Megan Farraday read the name printed in bold black lettering on the glass: "Daniels Wilderness Outfitters."

Anticipation coursed through her veins as she leaned a shoulder against the door and stepped inside. The room was dark after the brightness of the morning sun. Megan paused for a moment to tip the large owl sunglasses up on top of her head and get her bearings. A hush gradually fell over the small room that served as a waiting area as well as an office.

Men were clustered in groups of three or four, slouched on the two vinyl sofas or leaning casually against the paneled walls. Coffee steamed from the plastic cups in their hands. They wore their orange hats like badges, the unmistakable identification of a hunter. All heads turned her way and not a whisper of conversation lingered in the air. The atmosphere had suddenly become heavy.

Megan was very much aware that her presence was the cause of the chain reaction. She was also aware that ordinarily, when she entered a room, everyone didn't stop what they were doing to take notice of her. But all eyes were on her, making no attempt to disguise the speculation in their glances. Expressions ran the full gamut from surprised to curious, appraising to insulting. She was trespassing on their territory—male territory. They didn't quite know how to take it. Fortunately Megan did. Independent and headstrong, she was used to being in places or situations where others thought she didn't belong.

"Good morning, gentlemen." Her bright, smiling glance encompassed the entire room as she tried to set the tone before anyone else had the chance. If she addressed them as gentlemen, perhaps they would be.

"Good morning." Orange flashed about the

room as the hunters nodded a deep-chorused greeting.

There was no one ahead of her at the reservation counter, so Megan walked over to it, conscious of the loud, hollow sound of her heels on the worn planked floor.

"Yeah?" A bespectacled old man looked up from the notebook lying open on the counter in front of him. His gravelly voice matched the craggy, weathered look in his features. Of all the men, this one seemed the least interested in what she was doing there.

"I have a reservation for this morning—"

"Name?" It was a gruff request for the information Megan had been about to supply, before she was interrupted.

"Farraday," she replied evenly and leaned an elbow on the tall counter while the old man flipped through a box of index cards.

"What was the name again?" His frowning glance studied the card he had extracted.

"Farraday, M. Farraday." She repeated the name slowly.

"Then I guess this is it." Bony fingers reached to scratch the tanned baldness of his head. A puzzled look crossed his face, his interest heightened slightly. "It says here, 'number in party— one.'" It might have been phrased as a statement, but there was a rising inflection of a question.

It was a question Megan had anticipated. "That's right, just me." With cool nonchalance, she swung her purse off her shoulder and onto the counter. "What do I owe you?" Finding a pen, she held it between her teeth while she rummaged through the clutter in her bag for her checkbook.

The old man seemed to take the hint. Megan didn't want her plans to be made into an issue, especially when she had such a captive audience. He slid a copy of the charges to her, then pressed the button on the intercom.

"Twenty-eight's here," he barked into the speaker of the box.

Megan tore off the completed check and handed it to him.

"I don't know why you'd be wantin' to go out there all by yourself." As he peered at her over his glasses, there seemed to be a softening in his manner, concern, perhaps. Then he shrugged it away. "But I guess that's your own business."

Megan didn't disagree. She watched him examine the information on her check. Satisfied, he lifted his faded blue eyes back to her. "Okay, M. Farraday, your number's twenty-eight. Grab yourself a cup of coffee and wait for your number to be called."

"Thank you." Megan turned around to face fifteen pairs of eyes watching her. They watched while she walked to the coffee pot and poured the hot liquid into a plastic cup. Then they watched her bring the cup to her lips and slowly sip the boiling brew. It was a little unnerving.

"Did I hear right?" A rugged-looking man in a plaid shirt and orange hat standing near her broke the silence. "You're going into the wilderness alone?"

"You heard right." There was a smile, but it

was strained. Her patience was wearing thin as far as explanations were concerned. Too many hours had already been wasted explaining and arguing with friends and relatives who didn't think she should be making this trip. It was her decision, and she was tired of defending it.

"Aren't you just a little bit afraid? Those woods are full of wild animals." His tone was slightly condescending.

"If she gets scared, she can sleep in my tent." The remark came from someone behind her.

She didn't turn to see who the comedian was. A snicker sounded here and there. Long curling lashes came down to conceal the annoyance that darkened Megan's green eyes. When she met the hunter's gaze again, her eyes revealed nothing. Her smile was aloof, yet provocative.

"No, I'm not afraid. The wilderness isn't the only place you find wild animals." Turning slightly, she glanced behind her as the room exploded with guffawing male laughter.

"Twelve, thirteen." The shouted numbers carried above the din.

Two men with clipboards were standing in front of the reservation counter. When the noise died down enough to speak in normal tones, they introduced themselves as pilots and repeated the numbers called a moment ago. Ten of the hunters, including the more boisterous ones Megan had talked to, followed the pilots out the side door.

Their departure left room on one of the two mismatched vinyl couches. Megan sat down, crossing a slender leg over the opposite knee. The man at the other end of the couch was using the rectangular coffee table as a footstool. Megan set her half-filled cup near the edge. Lifting an ashtray that overflowed with cigarette butts, she pulled a magazine from atop the disheveled pile. A restless impatience set her foot in a pendulum motion.

"Twenty-eight." The deep male voice seized her attention with the number she'd been waiting to hear.

Her jade-green eyes darted a look upward at the man standing near the door. He was tall, easily reaching the six-foot mark or possibly surpassing it by an inch or two. A muscled chest and broad shoulders tapered to lean masculine hips and corded thighs. His features were strongly cut and sun-bronzed, handsome but with more emphasis on ruggedness and virility. His hair was casually tamed, rumpled by a playing wind. It fell across his forehead in dark, nearly black disarray.

But it was his eyes that drew Megan's attention. There was a certain boldness in the way his smoke-gray glance was making a thorough inspection of her, taking in every feminine aspect. The look was in no way demeaning or leering, so it was impossible for Megan to take offense. She interpreted the appraisal as a compliment and smiled a little absently to acknowledge it. Her mind was already racing ahead, anxious to depart.

As she tossed the magazine on the table and

started to rise, she was vaguely aware that the man's gaze had left her and was now making a sweep of the five remaining men.

"Twenty-eight?" It was a question this time, slightly impatient because he'd had to repeat it.

"That's me." She didn't consciously inject that note of challenge into her voice, but it was there just the same. She saw the mocking gleam in those gray eyes and guessed the man was mentally quirking an eyebrow at the information, although his expression didn't flicker once. Crossing the room, she grasped the hand he extended in greeting.

"I'm Colt Daniels, your pilot." His smile was one of professionalism, contradicting the male interest he had shown only a moment before.

"Megan Farraday." She shook his hand, liking the strength of his grip.

"Shall we?" A shove of the glass door swung it open and he braced an arm against it to hold the position. The hand with the clipboard made a wide sweep to motion her past him.

An extensive dock ran the length of the building and beyond. Three floatplanes in various colors were secured to the dock by sturdy ropes. Two of them were being loaded. Megan recognized the men assisting as the ones she had seen earlier in the office. Mounds of gun cases, fishing poles, tackle boxes and supplies slowly disappeared inside the yawning cavities of the planes.

"Where's your gear?" That was one thing the pilot needed to know before they went any farther. Megan wrinkled her nose, chagrined that she had forgotten all about her luggage in the excitement of the moment.

"It's in the van out front." Turning slightly, she pointed a finger. "The resort van picked me up at the airport. The driver said it would be all right to leave it there."

Amusement twitched at the corners of his mouth. "Hey, Emil," Colt Daniels called to one of the dock boys helping with the loading. "You and Jack get Miss Farraday's gear out of the van and load it in my plane." The two Indian boys raced down the wide dock in ready compliance with his orders.

"I'm docked on the end." The pilot struck out in the indicated direction with Megan taking longer strides than usual to keep pace with him.

"You said your name was Daniels. Is this your company?" It hadn't registered until now that he had the same name as the one printed on the door.

"Yeah, I'm the boss." Despite the casual way he answered her question, there was an unmistakable pride of ownership in his friendly glance.

Megan arched an eyebrow. "I'm impressed. The boss is flying me in personally." A sparkle lit her eyes, green and mischievous.

Colt Daniels flashed her a lazy grin. "I don't mind telling you I've never flown a woman into the bush country—by herself, that is."

"Well, Cowboy, that makes two of us, because I've never flown into the bush country, period." A laugh accompanied the admission.

He looked more like a cowboy than a pilot, she decided. His jeans were worn soft to hug his thighs. The pearl snaps of his blue flannel shirt were undone low at the neck to reveal coarse, dark chest hairs curling at the gap. A suede vest and western boots completed the picture.

"Touché." He tipped his dark head in deference to her claim.

The yellow floatplane was directly in front of them now. Bobbing on the rippling surface of Rainy Lake, it tugged at the ropes that anchored it securely to the dock. It seemed almost as eager to get started as Megan was.

The two dock boys were but a few minutes behind them, pushing a hand truck stacked high with her belongings. They began loading. Amusement danced in Colt Daniels' gray eyes and twitched around his mouth, deepening the slash lines at the corners without curving into a smile. Megan wondered what the joke was, until she followed his glance to the matching powder-blue luggage, portable typewriter and radio, cosmetic bag and case of mineral water that vanished into the small aircraft. Her "gear" differed greatly from the duffel bags and hunting equipment the men brought.

With everything stowed safely in the luggage compartment, Megan buckled herself into the passenger seat. Colt Daniels buckled his seatbelt and prepared for takeoff.

He taxied away from the shore and headed into the wind. There was a sudden rush of exhilaration as the plane skimmed the surface of the water and lifted off. This was a new experience for Megan and she reveled in it, trying to commit sensations and impressions to memory.

A steady climb took them high over the Rainy Lake region of Ontario, Canada. From this unique vantage point, the panoramic view was spectacular. The red-oranges and yellow-golds of autumn exploded across the landscape, the reflections blending into the vast expanse of water receding beneath them.

"Air time is an hour and ten minutes. You might as well relax."

The sound of Colt's voice reverted her attention back inside. Entranced with the scene stretching below them, she hadn't realized she was gripping the arms of her seat so tightly. White-knuckle flying was not her usual mode. She laughed, a little embarrassed.

"I'm not afraid," she assured him. "Just excited that I'm finally on my way. There have been times when it didn't seem like this would ever happen. I can hardly wait to get there and get started."

He glanced at her, briefly scanning her face. Turning back to the front, he absently adjusted his sunglasses. "I couldn't help but notice you didn't bring a rifle—or a fishing rod." After a moment, he faced her again. "If you don't mind my asking, what exactly is it you can't wait to get started doing? Other than the two things I just mentioned, there's not a whole lot to do where you're going."

"I suppose I do look out of place among all

these sportsmen," she conceded, then decided to explain despite her earlier aversion to doing so. Her reluctance was disintegrating with Colt Daniels' friendly interest. "I'm a novelist. I came up here from Los Angeles to get inspiration for my new book."

"You're on location, so to speak."

She nodded. "I like to do thorough research." A smile played around her mouth. "Thorough" was almost an understatement. Absolute authenticity was already her trademark, even if she had only one published novel to her credit.

"You couldn't just do your research at the library like everyone else," he mocked dryly.

"No. No, I couldn't." For her, it was more than learning dusty facts and dry statistics. "But you wouldn't understand." Few did, and fewer yet were interested enough to try.

"Maybe not." He admitted the possibility with an invisible shrug. "Why don't you explain it to me anyway?"

Megan hesitated, chewing a thumbnail. Then her gaze traveled out across the horizon, looking without seeing. "I guess it's a matter of total absorption. I need to feel what my characters are feeling, experience as much of their situation as I can." There was a brief silence before she went on. A new intensity darkened her eyes, hinting strongly of the passion she had for her work. "I want to bring my characters to life. When they hurt, I want to feel it in the pit of my stomach." Unconsciously she brought a fist firmly against her stomach. "When they're happy, I want to capture that joy. And when they love, I want it to be so real to me that the depth of it will be transmitted onto a piece of paper and whoever reads it will feel—something." A softness enveloped her features. "It will have made an impression. It will have mattered." Her moving glance encountered Colt's studious gaze, shaded but not hidden by the tinted lenses of his sunglasses.

"Too idealistic?" she asked, but didn't give him a chance to reply. "Maybe so, but I think that's what made my first novel an overnight success," Megan theorized. "In my twenty-four years I have not had the experience, nor do I have the genius, of a Hemingway. I believe *The Realm* is on the bestseller list only because it commands feeling."

With a shake of his head, Colt loudly expelled a long breath.

"What was that for?" she asked defensively. She had gone overboard, as usual. It was always that way when she talked about her work. "You think I'm a little crazy, don't you?" She was wishing very hard that she hadn't told him anything.

"Yep." Contained amusement laced the drawled agreement.

"What can I expect?" she bristled. "From someone who probably hasn't read a book in the last hundred years." Her reaction was always immediate and always defensive where her work was concerned. She loved to write and unconsciously expected everyone else to revere her chosen profession as much as she did. Her logical mind told her that wasn't fair, but it wasn't always easy to listen.

"A hundred years, huh?" Instead of taking offense at the jibe, Colt Daniels laughed, a deep, rumbling sound that melted through her indignation.

It was contagious. Soon Megan was laughing right along with him, her natural sense of humor returning. For the first time in the last couple of days, she felt herself begin to relax. While the pilot's attention was focused ahead, Megan took the opportunity to really look at him. The overall impression of sheer maleness remained, but there were a few details she had missed. The lines that were permanently grooved into his lean cheeks seemed to be waiting for his reckless smile to bring them into play. His profile was strongly cut, and it added to the inherent boldness of his nature. Megan had a sudden urge to brush the thick strands of dark hair from his forehead.

She looked away abruptly, the thought rocking through her senses. It was immediately followed by a burst of self-directed irritation. During the next month, there would not be time for men. She was here to work. She had a deadline to meet. Even back in Los Angeles, the men she dated came second to her career. There weren't many who were willing to settle for that arrangement, and that kept her from forming any lasting relationships. It was just as well, because Megan had long ago decided that a man would never rob her of a chance for a fulfilling career. And there were too many cases that proved it was impossible to have both.

Colt noticed her silence. "I don't think you're crazy because of your work." He clarified that point. "Your dedication is admirable. I do think you're crazy to stay at the outpost by yourself, though. And I'm probably crazier yet, for flying you in." He raked his fingers through his hair, as if he had sensed her impulse to do the same.

"Why do you say that?" she asked with a frown.

"Look around you." A wave of his hand went along with the instruction.

Megan did. She saw a vast land cloaked magestically in the colors of fall. Winding fingers of water snaked off in a multitude of directions, winking in the sun. The view was breathtaking, but Megan didn't understand what Colt wanted her to see. It all looked the same. Very little had changed since they'd left civilization behind.

"I don't see anything." She shrugged in confusion.

"Exactly. This is the wilderness, Miss Farraday. Can you imagine what it would be like to get lost out there?" The way he drew in breath, then exhaled with a slow shake of his head made it plain that it wasn't a position he would like to be in.

This time when Megan looked out the window it was with new eyes. She saw the total isolation of the raw and wild terrain. "I'll stay close to the cabin." It was a promise to herself as well as to Colt Daniels.

"It would be a good idea." He nodded thoughtfully. "I usually don't worry too much about someone getting lost. There are always several people in a party and they can look out for each other. But you being here all alone . . ." He didn't need to finish his statement and Megan didn't need to be warned twice.

"Yes," she agreed quickly. "I see what you mean."

"And you'll have to exercise a little extra caution in everything you do. If you should happen to get yourself injured, you can't just pick up the phone and call for help." As he spoke, his attention was fixed on some point off to the left. He didn't look at her.

"I know that," she assured him. "But the risk of my being injured isn't any greater than that of any of the hunters." Still, a note of apprehension crept into her voice.

"True enough," Colt conceded. "But that does bring up another point that concerns me."

"What?" She almost hated to ask.

"The hunters have guns . . . you don't."

"I don't see that as a problem since I'm not planning to do any hunting," Megan pointed out.

"I was thinking more along the lines of self-defense." He slid her a side glance, then returned his gaze to the front. "What if you come face to face with a moose . . . or a bear?"

Her head turned sharply to regard his serious expression. "Animals avoid people, don't they?

I've always heard the scent of a human would keep them from coming near a camp."

"I'll admit that the possibility is remote." A short silence followed the admission while Colt Daniels studied the many dials and gauges. "There have been cases, though."

Megan's laugh wasn't as natural as she would have liked. "Why do I get the feeling you're trying to scare me off?"

The sunglasses had slipped down a little on the straight bridge of his nose. Colt adjusted them before he answered. "You have a right to be informed of any potential danger. These are things you'll find out soon enough anyway."

"If you do this with all of your customers, I'm surprised you still have a business to run." Then she noticed the quirking movement at the side of his mouth and realized he was trying not to smile. "Or am I the only one who gets this advance warning?"

The lazy curving of his mouth confirmed her suspicion. "Let's just say I'd rather you change your mind now before we unload all your gear than afterward. It saves wear and tear on the back."

Pride stiffened her posture as it began to register that Colt Daniels was only humoring her, expecting she would lose her nerve and back out at the last minute. If anything, his warning had served as proof that this trip was necessary to capture the element of reality she was striving for.

"I won't change my mind," she stated firmly. "I

will be staying the full month, Mister Daniels. Just like I planned."

"The name's Colt," he corrected. "Unless you prefer Cowboy." His grin took on a roguish quality to match the glint in his eye. "I guess if I can't talk you out of it, I'd better land this plane."

"You mean we're here?" She looked out the window for something that would signify that they had reached their destination.

"Just ahead." He nodded to the front.

The first indication that they had arrived was the pier jutting out onto the water. Her gaze followed it to the rocky shoreline and then on to the cabin located a short distance inland. Nearly concealed by the trees, it was little wonder she hadn't seen the cabin from the air.

They landed smoothly, without incident. Colt's experience and ability as a pilot were evident in the ease with which he maneuvered the floating plane to the dock. After he had secured it, he offered Megan a steadying hand as she climbed from the shifting transport.

The luggage was unloaded and the supply of food was piled onto the dock. If Colt wasn't yet convinced of her intention to stay, he didn't say anything. With the two largest suitcases and several smaller items stuffed under his arms, he started down the narrow pier toward the cabin. Megan picked up the small suitcase and her portable typewriter and followed.

The lower half of the cabin walls was constructed of plywood. The upper portion was canvas, including the roof. A stove pipe protruded through the top. It differed slightly from Megan's preconceived image of a rustic log cabin with a stone fireplace. But that wasn't something she admitted to Colt.

There was the thud of a heavy suitcase being set on the wooden stoop and the rattle of a doorknob. Then Colt was pushing it open on hinges that squeaked with the motion.

"There are still a few places where you don't have to lock your doors." He tossed the comment over his shoulder as he entered the single large room.

Four bunks, stacked two-high, lined one wall. A kitchen, of sorts, occupied the opposite wall. There was one window made of flexible plastic. Next to it sat a wooden table and four chairs. In the center of the room, a potbelly stove stood guard.

Colt set the luggage down near the bunks. "Home sweet home," he mocked, curiously watching her reaction. "It's not exactly a castle."

Megan knew he expected her to be taken aback by the complete lack of anything remotely resembling a luxury. But for her purposes, this cabin was ideal.

"I think it's cute." She defended her temporary home with a smile that was genuinely bright in its approval.

"Cute?" Judging by the disbelief in his voice, it wasn't a description he would have applied. Then exasperation took over his expression and he ran a hand through his hair, adding to its already rumpled condition. It gave him a rakish look. "Cute, huh?"

"I believe that was the word I used." Megan made it clear that her opinion remained unchanged.

"I don't know why that surprises me," Colt said dryly. "What else could I expect from someone who shows up in a silk blouse and high-heeled hiking boots and thinks she's ready to rough it. You might think this place is 'cute' for a day or two, but believe me, the novelty will wear off quick."

Megan bristled at the injustice of his remark, knowing that he refused to take her seriously because she was a woman. No one would think twice if she were a man. There was a definite shimmer of defiance in her green eyes and a challenging tilt to her chin.

"Regardless of what you think, I am not out here on a lark. I have come all the way from Los Angeles for this experience, so I'm not likely to change my mind because of a few inconveniences."

"All I'm saying is, I don't think you realize what you're up against." His tone softened.

"I think I do. But if not, I can handle it. I'm a big girl now." As soon as the last sentence was out of her mouth she regretted it. It invited his lingering gaze to travel up and down her length in an assessment of the figure that proved her statement. Megan was annoyed with herself for making the remark and even more annoyed with the way her heartbeat quickened and the breath seemed to catch in her throat. A change of subject was needed.

"Is there any coffee?" It was an excuse and they both knew it, but it didn't keep Megan from following through. She avoided the knowing gleam in his eyes as she walked to the single cupboard and began a search of its contents.

"There's some in the box of supplies on the dock," he replied with a calm unconcern Megan envied.

"Good." The dented aluminum percolator she found clanged a little more loudly than necessary when she set it on the sink drainboard. "I'll go get it." She stepped past him and out the door, the breeze cooling her heated face.

Halfway down the path, Colt came up behind her. "You forgot something." Amusement glittered in his eyes. A red plastic bucket hung from two fingers, swaying in the breeze.

"What's that for?" She frowned at the bucket, then at Colt.

"Water."

"Water?" Her frown deepened. "Oh, water." It slowly dawned on her. There was no running water in the cabin—no plumbing of any kind. "The sink . . . I just assumed . . ."

"The drain works." His mouth slanted into a smile that was about half and half sympathetic and smug. "I'll get the water from the well. You'll find the can of coffee in the smallest box."

"Okay."

Megan started toward the supplies stacked on the dock. Discovering that there was no running water left her a little dazed. That was something she had taken for granted, a necessity rather than a luxury. Even if she'd known about the well, she would have assumed it would have an inside pump. Apparently that was a luxury, too.

She was nearly to the jumble of boxes before she realized Colt was a couple of steps behind her. Locating a small box, she turned to Colt to verify that it was the one containing the coffee. But he was walking past her to the end of the dock. Megan watched while he leaned over the edge and scooped a bucket of water from the lake. His grin was wicked as he strolled back to where she stood.

Megan laughed in spite of herself—or, more accurately—because of herself. "That's a mighty big well, Cowboy," she teased in her best Texas drawl.

"Yes, ma'am," he played along. "That there's the sweetest water this side of the Rio Grande." Laughter rolled from his throat, rich and smooth to blend with hers.

"Seriously, though," Megan said, tipping her head to one side, "isn't it dangerous to drink lake water?"

"Not up here," Colt denied with a trace of pride. "It's fresh and pure, the way nature intended."

"It's beautiful here." The air was crisp and

pleasantly scented with pine. She took a deep, testing breath. "No smog!" she reported.

A lazy indulgence settled itself on the lean male features of Colt Daniels. "Are you going to stand there breathing or are we going to have that cup of coffee?" Cupping a hand under her elbow, he steered her up the worn path to the cabin.

Chapter Two

The coffee perking on the stove filled the room with a strong, tantalizing aroma. Two plain white mugs sat waiting on the table.

"It's done." A chair leg scraped on the warped plywood floor as Colt pushed back from the table and walked to the stove.

"How do you know?" With an elbow resting on the edge of the table, Megan twined her manicured fingers in her thick, toffee-colored hair. Her question revealed more than a casual interest for such a simple task as making a pot of coffee.

The way Colt was eyeing her, he must have thought so, too. "By the smell," he said. "It doesn't take long to know when it's just right."

"This will take some getting used to," she commented idly. "I've never made coffee from scratch before."

"From scratch?" Colt murmured with a mocking lift of his eyebrows. After pouring the clear brown liquid into the ceramic mugs he returned the pot to the burner.

"Yes, I was taught that to make coffee, you plug in the coffee maker and wait for the little red light to come on. That's just one of the many small details I need to know to make my story authentic." She gingerly sipped from her steaming cup, surprised at the rich difference in flavor. "Umm, you make good coffee." It burned deliciously down her throat.

"It's the water," he replied modestly. "No chemicals to alter the taste. There are a lot of people who have never tasted a cup of pure coffee."

Megan watched him relax against the chair back, noticing the ruggedness that made him seem a natural part of the surroundings. "I suppose you've spent a lot of time in these cabins yourself."

"Yes, I have." Sinew and muscle interplayed in his brown forearm below the rolled sleeve as he lifted the cup to his lips. "They're usually reserved during the hunting season, but I often stay out here when business slows down."

"What do you do out here?"

"Well, I fish . . . hunt . . . and sometimes just relax. It's so quiet and peaceful—no phones ringing. I just kick back and do absolutely nothing." A grin spread slowly across his face and Megan had the impression he was reliving those simple pleasures.

"Do you mean you stay out here all by your-self?" Her feigned surprise was a mocking re-minder of the way he had warned her against staying alone.

"That's different," he stated without explana-tion.

It was. Megan could see that now. She was also beginning to see that his objections to her being there were based on her inexperience, not her sex.

"Maybe." She was still reluctant to concede. "Tell me. Have you ever seen a bear?" The question had been nagging at her since her ar-rival.

"Maybe three or four times. They're not that easy to find," he admitted with a low chuckle. Seeing the accusing light in her eyes, he rushed on to explain. "That doesn't mean they're not out there. There have been a couple of isolated incidents. They were after food. You have to keep everything in the refrigerator."

"I'll remember that." It was a quick response.

His sharp glance jerked to her face. "Does that mean you're staying?"

"I told you I was," she answered, meeting his look squarely.

"That was before you knew just how primitive the conditions were," he reminded her. "Look, I can arrange a room for you at the resort and you can fly out here every morning on the early run and back each evening."

Megan was touched by the trouble he was willing to take to make her stay more comfortable. She wasn't used to men being so protective of her. Her father had died when she was very young and her stepfather had traveled a great deal, insisting that her mother accompany him much of the time. There was a housekeeper, but mostly Megan had been left to fend for herself. It resulted in the development of a strong sense of independence, a trait she had been forced to acquire and now wasn't willing to relinquish.

"I appreciate what you're trying to do, but I need to be here." She refused his offer gently but firmly.

"What's the difference?" he asked. "You can't work twenty-four hours a day anyway. If you check into the resort, you'd have a good bed to sleep in, hot water, room service—"

"Don't tempt me," she broke in, because it all sounded so good. "I have to stay."

"Why?" He frowned.

"Because I have to identify with the heroine in my story. The girl has been kidnapped and left alone in an old hunting cabin while the three men attempt to extort money from her wealthy father," she explained, briefly sketching in the plot. "So maybe you can see why I had to come out here. If I hadn't I would have given Sally a cozy log cabin and the unrealistic comforts of running water and probably a real bed." A laugh bubbled from her throat. "You weren't far off from my idea of roughing it."

Several silent seconds ticked by while Colt absorbed what she'd told him. Then he was looking at his watch and pushing back from the table. "In that case, I'd better bring those supplies up here."

Within half an hour, Megan had everything put away. The shelves were well stocked with canned goods, and everything else was in the propane refrigerator. There was enough food for about ten days. Someone would fly in to replenish the supply.

When Megan offered Colt another cup of coffee, he glanced at his watch again. "No, thanks. I need to get going. Come on down to the dock. There are a couple of things you need to know before I leave."

One of them was how to operate the aluminum fishing boat. Colt wasn't satisfied to issue verbal instructions only. He accompanied Megan on a test run to make sure she understood. Once her competence was established, he tied the boat to the dock and she walked with him to the plane. Gleaming yellow in the sunlight, it shifted under his weight as he climbed inside. A moment later, he emerged with a leather rifle case in one hand and a box of cartridges in the other.

"I want you to keep this with you, just in case." He thrust the rifle into her hands, but she didn't take it, pushing it back instead.

"I really don't think I'll be needing this."

"A precautionary measure." His look was stern, unyielding on this point. Removing the rifle from its case, he inserted three shells.

"I thought you weren't supposed to leave a gun

loaded when it isn't being used." Megan remembered the safety instructions she'd heard.

"You aren't," Colt confirmed the wisdom of that and handed the gun to Megan. "But since I'm fairly certain you've never used one before, we'd better have a lesson."

His guess was an accurate one, but Megan wasn't thrilled about increasing her knowledge of firearms. The gun metal was cold and heavy in her hands, its power making her shiver inwardly.

She swallowed, a little nervous. "You want me to shoot it?"

Colt's serious expression melted into a grin, that hint of dry humor returning to his eyes, nearly the same gray color as the gun metal but infinitely warmer. "You'd better learn how to shoot it, unless you'd rather let an attacker get close enough to hit him with it."

"Okay." She laughed. "What do I do?"

"I'll help you on the first shot so you can get the feel of it."

Moving to stand behind her, his arms came around to the front, guiding her hands to position the rifle properly. "The main thing to remember is to hold the wood stock tightly against your shoulder." The instruction was issued in a low voice next to her ear. "There will be a little bit of a kick, so expect that and you won't have any trouble."

Megan was conscious of his male body, touching her in some places and so close that she could feel the warmth of him even where there wasn't any actual contact. It was disturbing and reassuring at the same time. Unsure of how much 'kick' to expect from the rifle, she knew the muscled wall of his chest would help to absorb any shock.

When he told her how to aim, how to close one eye and look through the scope with the other, the rough-shaven line of his jaw brushed the softness of her cheek. The spicy tang of his after-shave mingled with the leathery smell of his suede vest and the pungent odor of gun oil, filling her lungs with every breath and awakening her senses to full perception.

"Now, aim at one of those trees across the lake."

His breath ruffled her hair as he spoke, making it suddenly difficult for Megan to concentrate on what he was saying. Her heartbeat nearly overrode the quiet sound of his voice. A shot echoed across the lake a full second before Megan realized she had pulled the trigger—but not without Colt's forefinger applying a slight pressure on hers.

"Think you've got it?" he asked before he released her.

Megan nodded, certain that her inner disturbance would be revealed in her voice. Then Colt was stepping back, seemingly unaffected by the close contact.

"Try it by yourself this time." He watched while she squeezed off two more rounds, then had her load the rifle without his assistance. "I have another party to fly in this afternoon." The information fell somewhere between an excuse and an apology for leaving. "I hope it's a little more conventional than this run."

Megan felt her defenses start to bristle because she had enjoyed his company and had thought the feeling was mutual. "I imagine it will be." A stiffness edged her words.

"Yes, but not nearly as interesting." The lazy charm of his smile was leveled on her as if to say the extra time he had spent had not been wasted. "Either myself or one of the other pilots will be flying over this area at least once a day. If you need anything at all, take one of the white dish towels and hang it on that tall post at the end of the dock. Everyone in the area recognizes a white flag as an SOS, so someone will stop."

Remembering his earlier implication that she would be completely isolated, without any means of communication, Megan said in an accusing tone, "Gee, that's almost as easy as picking up the telephone, isn't it?" But even while she taunted him, she recognized that his scare tactics had only been a protective measure. How could she hold that against him?

"Almost," he agreed easily and with amusement. "Don't hesitate to fly the white flag, even if you just want someone to talk to. It can get pretty lonely out here."

"I don't think I'll get lonely." She paused deliberately, a mischievous jade glitter in her eyes. "Not with Nick coming along in a couple of days to keep me company."

His gaze narrowed to glide over her face like

smooth charcoal, hard and dark gray. "Nick? You didn't mention that someone would be joining you."

Megan thought she detected a sour note, although it was masked by a cool professionalism. "Oh, didn't I tell you about Nick?" She blinked. "He's the hero in my story. When I get started, he'll be as real to me as you are." A fine tension stretched between them as her eyes momentarily locked with his. It forced her to tack a silent "almost" onto the end of her statement.

There was no humor in his look when his gaze focused on the full curve of her lips. They parted instinctively, without her being fully aware of it.

"Of course," he said dryly. "I should have guessed."

Turning, he walked to the yellow plane to deftly untie the anchoring cables. "Au revoir, Miss Megan Farraday, writer-at-large. I wish you and . . . whoever . . . a pleasant stay." Something had made the mocking farewell insincere. With deerlike agility, he was in the plane and striking up the engine. There was a brief salute before he reached somewhere above him to retrieve the sunglasses he had hung there earlier and then placed them on the bridge of his nose to shield his eyes against the glaring sun that could blind him to another aircraft.

Megan stood on the deserted dock, gazing after the small plane as its drone became barely distinguishable and then disappeared. The quiet and serenity of the lake seemed to have never been touched by the big yellow bird or the vitally handsome man that sat at the controls. The solitude and pressing stillness were almost eerie in their effect after the hustle and bustle of Los Angeles only hours before. She shrugged off the shiver that ran its icy fingers down her spine. "It's a little late to get cold feet," she chided herself and turned to walk back up to the cabin—and her work.

The only table in the cabin was monopolized by the typewriter. There was also a stack of paper, a can of sharpened pencils, a thick dictionary and a notebook containing a tentative plot outline. Basic incidents and assorted details had been filled in, although a definite ending was as yet undecided.

A mound of wadded-up papers littered the cabin floor surrounding the table. Megan ripped another sheet from the typewriter to crumple it in frustration and add to the accumulating mess. The first couple of days had gone exceedingly well, but now she had come to an abrupt halt. Struggling was getting her nowhere, so she decided to get a good night's sleep. She would think better in the morning.

But the next day was no different. By nightfall, Megan was forced to face the truth. Writer's block! It had happened to her only once before and had lasted a miserable three weeks. With only three and a half weeks left at the cabin, she couldn't afford to spend three of it bound to the typewriter, wracking her brain for words and phrases that wouldn't come. A determination surfaced to work her way through it. She broke out a new bottle of mineral water, put another log in the stove and began again.

When dawn spread its shimmering rays on the lake, Megan was staring at another blank white sheet in her typewriter. The crumpled sheets it had replaced were piling up around her feet. It was hopeless. The harder she tried, the worse it got. Dejection slumped her shoulders as she poured a glass of orange juice and grabbed her jacket from the hook by the door. Daybreak was painting streaks on the lake's mirror surface when her tired steps echoed on the dock. There were many posts sticking up along the pier. She plopped down, using one of them as a backrest while she tried to concentrate on nothing but the magnificent sunrise before her. It was like a spectacular fireworks display—a private showing here, in the middle of the wilderness.

The air was fresh and clear and Megan drank it in, hoping to sweep the cobwebs from her mind. Thinking back on everything she'd heard about writer's block, she knew she was doing it all wrong. She was trying too hard. What was it that finally broke through the last time? A conscious effort to forget had pushed that unpleasant period from her mind, but now she forced the memories. After several minutes, she bolted upright, sitting cross-legged while her thoughts raced.

"That's it," she said aloud. Fatigue was instantly banished and a triumphant smile broke across her face as she remembered. "If you have a block and can no longer get a clear picture of your scene, act it out." That was it! That's what she'd done and it had worked. Perhaps it would work now. It was definitely worth a try.

The short distance back to the cabin was covered in a flash. Snatching the white dish towel from the hook, she jogged back down to the dock, where she tied the towel through the metal eye in the tallest post. Her breath was coming faster and her color was heightened when she sat back down to wait. It was difficult to say if it was from the short jog or the excitement of a possible solution to her problem. Probably a little of both.

An hour later, she was experiencing some second thoughts. True, it had worked before, but the circumstances were totally different. Then, the "acting out" or "going through the motions" involved only her own participation, not other people's. Certainly not Colt Daniels'. Could he possibly understand the dilemma she was facing? Would he even try? She started toward the white towel to disengage it from its hook where it waved in the breeze when another thought struck her. Deadline! Absurd as what she was planning to do might be, the possibility of losing three weeks, maybe even more, was even more absurd. She had a tight schedule to adhere to in order to meet her deadline. Three weeks' delay wouldn't fit in. No, she had to at least give this idea a shot. The white flag was still flying when she walked back up the gravel path.

Megan sat at the table, priming herself with fresh coffee to alleviate the traces of a sleepless night. Her green eyes thoroughly searched the patch of sky visible through the window. At the sound of an approaching small-engine aircraft, her search became more intense, her body taut with expectation. The yellow floatplane she was anticipating didn't materialize. Instead, a red plane with wheels rather than pontoons flew low over the white flag, tipping its wings to indicate that he understood the SOS and would notify an appropriate plane. Megan bit her lip nervously. She had assumed Colt would be the pilot to answer her signal.

She poured some warm water from the tea kettle into the wash basin and washed her face, then brushed her teeth. Between the coffee and the freshening up she felt almost as if she'd had a night's sleep. *Almost.* A touch of makeup and a brisk brushing of her gleaming caramel-brown hair made her feel like she was back in the human race. As she was changing her blouse, she heard the faint hum of another aircraft. Her heart was pumping faster. She hurriedly tucked the tails of her silk turquoise blouse into the waistband of some designer jeans. Peering out of the cabin window, her gaze scanned the small patch of cloudless blue sky. The motor noise was getting louder, but Megan still couldn't see from what or from where it was coming. Suddenly a movement caught her attention. The yellow floatplane was on the water, taxing up to the dock. It had red lettering on it. It was Colt Daniels'. If the plane hadn't been recognizable, the man climbing out of it definitely was. The broad shoulders and slim hips of the six-foot-plus physique certainly belonged to Colt Daniels, as did the dark hair and the agile athletic grace with which he moved. He anchored the wings and started toward the cabin.

"Oh, no, what have I done?" Megan whispered into her hands, pressed against her mouth. Colt was almost to the cabin, she could see him clearly. The chiseled, sun-bronzed features were wearing a curious expression, the gray of his eyes looked almost black. Lines were grooved into his lean cheeks, indicating how frequently he smiled, but he wasn't smiling now. *I can't go through with it!* Megan's cold feet were turning to ice. *Deadline!* That single word sounded loud and clear in her mind. Everything else became unimportant. Her cold feet were forgotten. She had a singleness of purpose when she stood back from the door waiting for Colt to enter the cabin. The deadline was all that mattered.

The wooden boards on the crude stoop creaked under Colt's weight. The knock at the door started her nerves jumping. When there was no response, he knocked louder. Megan kept silent. He knocked again, this time calling her name, a thread of concern in his tone. Megan watched the doorknob slowly turn; the moment she'd been waiting for was almost at hand. The pulse in her temples was hammering loudly. Her throat was dry. She swallowed hard. Then the door was swinging open with a creaking of its hinges.

The bright light from outside silhouetted the strong frame that nearly filled the opening. "Megan." His voice held an urgency, his eyes narrowed to adjust to the darkened interior of the cabin.

She stepped out from the shadows. "Colt, I'm so glad you're back!" She threw herself into his arms, but not before she glimpsed the look of surprise on his face. "I was so afraid." She clung to him.

He drew her close, comforting her. "What happened, Megan? What's the matter?"

She faked a sob. "I'm just so glad you are here. Please don't leave me again."

"Megan?" Colt loosened his hold so he could see her face. Before he could say or do anything and before she could lose her nerve, Megan kissed him full on the lips, tightening her arms around his neck to hold him there. His instinctive, stunned resistance was short-lived. He quickly became a willing and active participant in the charade. It startled Megan into releasing the pressure on his neck. But Colt made no move to let her go.

At first, Megan had begun concentrating on Colt's reactions—that initial shock, followed almost instantly by an instinct to protect and comfort. But something was happening to change that. Her own reactions were overpowering any desire or ability to make an analytical observation.

A heady warmth spread like quicksilver through her veins. Her hands were again applying pressure to the back of his neck, but Megan wasn't fully aware of it. She was aware of her lips moving against his in an automatic response generated by the stimulating feel of them.

His arm slid down the curve of her waist and around to tighten at the small of her back, shaping her more fully to his length. His flatly muscled build seared its imprint on her flesh, the heat from his body penetrating the barrier of clothes.

His other hand wound itself into the silky thickness of her hair as his mouth teased the softness of her lips to entice a heightened response. When she raised on tiptoe, Colt bent his head to increase the force and deepen the kiss.

An excitement she didn't want to feel was building steadily, rising and curling through her system. There was an intense willingness to stay where she was, in spite of the hundreds of alarm bells going off inside. This was all supposed to be for the sake of the book, nothing personal.

Yet Megan was forced to wonder if her writer's block hadn't come from an unconscious desire to see Colt Daniels again. The thought gave her the strength to drag her mouth from his, although it was a slow movement, drugging weakness still lingering.

Colt's arms remained circled around her waist when he finally managed to end the kiss, reluctant to let her go. There was a certain satisfaction in seeing that his breathing was disturbed, not coming as easily as it normally did. She wasn't the only one feeling the effects.

Her hands were braced on his forearms and

Megan pushed back, creating a space between them. She lifted her chin to meet the smoldering gray depths of his eyes, half concealed by spiky black lashes. She couldn't meet his gaze for long as a feeling of shame washed over her. She had used him. Funny, her motives had seemed justified a few moments earlier and now it all seemed like a cheap, selfish trick. Not so funny. She twisted out of his arms, turning her back to him.

"I'm sorry, Colt. I shouldn't have done that." A constriction in her throat made her voice husky.

"Hey, I'm not complaining." His low chuckle vibrated along her sensitized nerve ends. Then he was moving close behind her, his hands settling on her shoulders.

Megan shifted away from him, turning around but still unable to face him squarely. She stared at the second button of his red flannel shirt where his pulse throbbed in the exposed tanned hollow of his throat. "You don't understand. The whole thing was a hoax. I used you." It turned her stomach to see herself so callous. She hadn't even considered his feelings.

A short silence thickened the air while he studied her. "Use me some more," he murmured lazily. "I like being used."

When her gaze darted to his face, there was a seductive gleam in his smoke-gray eyes. A silly, crooked grin slanted the masculine mouth that had played such havoc with her senses. Megan had to laugh. She was whipping herself with the backlash of conscience and he hadn't minded the episode one bit. She hadn't either—except for the lack of honesty.

"Then I can safely assume that you're all right. You're not afraid?" Colt wanted to be certain of that.

"Right on both counts," Megan assured him.

"That leaves one thing, then. You were lonely for me. You don't have to apologize for that." There was a wicked glint in his eyes, playful and mischievous.

"When you hear the rest, you may not think it's so funny," Megan warned.

"Let's find out," he challenged.

Chapter Three

While Megan read through the half-dozen typed sheets of the troublesome scene, Colt relaxed in the hard-backed chair. His long legs were stretched in front of him, his hands folded across the hard muscles of his stomach.

"So," he said when she'd finished. "I was playing the part of Nick, kidnapper-turned-nice-guy, and you were Sally, alone and frightened in the cabin."

"Right." Megan nodded her agreement that the summary was correct.

"I still don't see how that brief incident could help you. It only lasted a few minutes and you've been stuck on the scene for two days," he mused and raised his coffee cup to his lips.

"I don't completely understand it myself. But I have a theory." Standing the papers on edge, she tapped them against the table top, then set them aside. "I believe it's next to impossible to write about something you can't see clearly, and I could not get a clear picture of how Nick would react when Sally threw herself into his arms and kissed him. I mean, she had only just met the man! And since I'm not a man, I couldn't imagine how one would take it."

The grooves around his mouth deepened in a sensual smile. "Now you know."

"Now I know." Remembered emotion charged the air as their eyes met. Megan looked away to stop the quivering sensations that were starting all over again. This tall, dark stranger was having an effect on her that she didn't need right now. There was a deadline to meet and Colt Daniels wasn't on her schedule. "And it made a difference in my story," she added quickly. "Nick and Sally's relationship will move along much different channels now. All because of that one moment."

Suddenly she felt self-conscious, as if she weren't talking about Nick and Sally at all. Meeting Colt's heavily lidded gaze, she was uncomfortably certain his thoughts were also traveling along those lines.

"Are you hungry?" She changed the subject and jumped to her feet. After the rotten trick she had played on him, the least she could do was offer to fix him something to eat before he left. Especially since he had taken the whole thing so well. "If you'll charcoal the steaks, I'll fix the salad," she bargained.

An eyebrow was lifted to mock her suggestion. "Steak and salad at ten in the morning?"

She laughed, knowing it must sound strange. But she couldn't remember ever being accused of falling in with the norm. "Since I've been up all night, I'm ready for a late supper." She sent him a twinkling look. "But I can fry some eggs to put with your steak and you can call it breakfast if it will make you feel any better."

"We'll compromise," Colt offered a solution. "Serve the salad and I'll call it lunch."

"Deal," she agreed.

"I'll light the grill." He picked up the bag of charcoal and the can of lighter fluid on his way out the door. To the left of the porch, a small wire grate rested atop a circle of good-sized rocks. That was the grill. Megan hadn't used it yet. She rarely took time to cook or eat a regular meal. But it didn't keep her from thoroughly enjoying one when she had the opportunity.

The steaks were cooked to medium-rare perfection and the salad was crisp. Colt finished a few minutes before Megan because she took time to savor every bite. He was watching her with amused interest when she finally pushed her empty plate aside.

"You have quite a flair for cooking." Her compliment was both sincere and a little bemused.

"You have quite a flair for eating," he teased in return.

Her expression became slightly affronted. "I hardly ever eat this much," she defended, knowing it was the good company that seemed to add to the flavor. She hated to eat alone. Which was probably why she usually just pieced and snacked on whatever was simplest, rather than prepare a solitary meal.

"Don't spoil my illusion," Colt advised. "I thought it was a nice switch to have 'dinner' with a woman who didn't gripe about the calories all the way through."

"So that was supposed to be a compliment." She challenged the remark that hadn't exactly come off as flattering.

"Of course." He drew back in mock dismay. "What else could it be?" Droll amusement robbed any innocence from his words. "Are you ready for coffee?" This time he changed the subject.

Megan let him off the hook. "Yes, it's all fixed. I'll just put it on the stove," she said when he started to rise. Colt just motioned her to stay where she was and walked over to light the gas burner under the dented pot.

"Thanks." A drowsiness began to claim her as she waited. The long hours without rest were slowly catching up with her and the comfortable fullness of her stomach added to her contented, lazy state. She thought of the soft velvet sofa in her apartment back home, then shifted her position on the hard wooden chair seat. A sigh broke from her lips.

"That was a sad sound," Colt commented on her wistful sigh. "Why?"

"Oh, it's nothing, really," she assured him. "I was just thinking about a sofa. These chairs seem to get harder by the minute."

"You're right." It was a quick agreement, voiced while he made a thoughtful survey of the room. He stood with his hands on his hips and Megan could almost hear the wheels turning in his head as he sized up the situation.

With a couple of giant strides, he was pulling the mattress off the two upper bunks, leaving one flat on the floor and folding the other lengthwise to wedge it behind the first. Then he was sliding the whole concoction against the wood frame of the lower bunk for a back support.

Megan watched with a trace of humor. "Aren't you resourceful?" And she meant it gratefully.

"Anything to keep my customers satisfied. I thought I proved that earlier." Tossing a quick grin over his shoulder, he carefully spread a woven Indian blanket over the makeshift sofa. He straightened and turned. "You were satisfied this morning, weren't you?" His expression was dead serious except for the roguish silver glimmer in his eyes.

"What kind of a question is that?" Megan laughed out loud to cover her embarrassment.

"If you weren't, I could make the necessary improvements. Satisfaction guaranteed." The natural male curve of his mouth slanted to make it a heady promise.

"No, your performance was satisfactory, thank you." Laughing, she managed to return the sexual banter even though the whole truth wasn't being told.

No, she wasn't satisfied with one kiss. It left her wanting more. She had caught herself several times during the day, watching his lips as he talked, remembering how they felt against hers. Again she had to remind herself that a man at this stage of the game would only complicate matters. Her career was too important to risk a diversion of her attention. But Colt's very presence seemed to demand it, triggering the warning signals. He was the kind of man she could fall in love with. She couldn't let that happen. There wasn't enough time or energy for the kind of commitment that entailed. As long as she was aware of what could happen, she could prevent it. So she told herself there was no reason for concern.

"The coffee smells like it's done," she announced several minutes later. "I'll get us a cup. We can have it on our new sofa." Her eyes twinkled with her smile to emphasize her appreciation of his efforts.

"It smells just right. You might make a camper yet," he said mockingly. "I'll put another log in the 'fireplace.'" Opening the door of the ornate potbellied stove, he poked another log inside.

Megan brought two steaming white mugs and offered one to Colt. They sat down together on the sofa he had made. By stretching their legs straight out in front of them and leaning against the back, they found it relatively comfortable. It seemed so to Megan. She was so fatigued that anything would have felt good as long as she could stretch out. They faced the woodstove. Flames licked at the tiny glass windows in its door, hypnotizing like a fireplace. The heat it radiated spread warmth around them like a protective cocoon. As it penetrated, Megan closed her eyes, totally relaxed.

"Megan." Colt's voice sounded far away to her. "Megan, are you asleep?" It wasn't much more than a whisper.

Fighting back the inviting twilight, Megan forced her eyelids open, focusing blurry-eyed on Colt. "No, I was just resting my eyes for a minute." She shook her head, feeling guilty for being a poor hostess.

"It's time I was going," he said gently. "You need some sleep."

"You don't have to leave." She pushed herself into an upright position, instantly contrite. "I promise I'll be better company." She struggled for an alertness that seemed strangely unattainable.

"Okay, okay," Colt agreed with a deep chuckle. "I'll stay for one more cup of coffee if you promise to relax and close your eyes." He could see she was so tired she wasn't thinking straight any more.

She gave him a wary look, her eyelids threatening to close. "All right, but I won't go to sleep," she assured him.

The last thing she saw was his smile before long, curling lashes swept the creamy smoothness

of her cheeks. She never knew how long Colt
stayed, watching her sleep in the waning afternoon light. Somewhere in her dreams he brushed
a kiss across her forehead.

It was late evening when she awakened, fully
clothed except for her shoes. She was stretched
full length on the sofa with a pillow under her
head and two warm blankets piled on top of her.
There was a moment of disorientation before she
remembered that Colt had been there. He must
have covered her. A warm glow began to spread,
adding to the heat trapped beneath the blankets.

Reluctantly, she tossed back the covers and
climbed out of bed, arching her spine and flexing
her muscles to loosen them up. There was enough
room on top of the woodstove to leave a tea kettle
of water constantly warming. Megan used it to
take a sponge bath and changed into a stylish but
comfortable light gray sweatsuit. She tied her
golden brown hair at the nape of her neck with a
red silk scarf.

Fully awake now, she began to notice some
changes in the cabin. The woodbox was stacked
high with split logs, the clean resinous smell of
new-cut wood in the air. Two plastic buckets were
standing on the counter near the sink, filled to the
brim with fresh lake water. There was a bemused
smile edging her mouth as Megan walked to the
typewriter, anxious to get back to work.

A typewritten note was propped against the
keyboard. Her smile deepened and split into a
wide grin as she read:

Megan,

Thanks for the lunch. Glad I could help with your book.

Colt

P.S. You owe me one!

She had to chuckle at that last line. "You're right, Cowboy, I do."

It was only later that she realized just how much she owed him. Her work was sailing along, seemingly effortless. What a contrast. She breezed through the rest of the day, falling into bed early, tired but pleased.

The fall weather had changed into a beautiful Indian summer. It was warm enough that Megan had taken to sunbathing on the dock during the late morning or early afternoon. She took along a notebook to jot down ideas. That seemed to justify the time she spent away from the type-writer.

At nearly noon on a hot day, Megan spread a large yellow beach towel on the planked surface of the dock. She rubbed a generous coating of suntan oil onto the exposed areas of her skin—all that she could reach. Lying on her back, she soaked up the soothing warmth of the sun's rays. The blue and yellow Hawaiian print bikini left all but a minute portion of her softly feminine curves to the mercy of the elements. She was totally absorbed in her thoughts as they wove in and around the characters of her book.

The yellow plane was nearly on top of her before she was aware of it. It came in low, tipping its wings in a friendly hello. Raising up on an elbow, she shaded her eyes with one hand. It was Colt. She waved as he picked up altitude and began a wide circle. In a couple of minutes he was back, swooping down at a steep angle. That and the excessive rate of speed made a safe landing impossible. It looked as if he was going to hit the dock. Cold panic clutched at her throat and her hands instinctively flew to cover her face.

The roar of the engine was loud in her ears for a heart-stopping moment. Then its volume decreased and Megan knew he had realized his error and taken the plane up to try it again. When she looked through the spaces between her fingers, Colt was nowhere in sight. The drone was fading into the distance rather than indicating another approach.

There was confusion mixed in with her delayed sigh of relief. Then her gaze focused on something in the lake, something Colt must have dropped because the surface had been clear and glassy a moment before. Now there were ripples ringing out from the two-liter plastic bottle bobbing on the water. She scooted to the edge of the dock, but the bottle was beyond her reach.

Climbing into the fishing boat brought her closer, but not close enough. She disengaged an oar from its bracket and attempted to guide the floating bottle closer. It looked like there was a note inside. After a few painstaking tries, Megan realized she was only pushing it farther away. She spotted a long-handled dip net in the bottom of the boat. Picking it up, she went to the bow and gingerly leaned out across the water. She was touching it! Only an inch more and she'd have it.

She leaned to stretch that extra inch and the boat tipped. She drew in a shocked breath as her sun-heated skin hit the water with an icy splash. She came up sputtering and shivering, laughing and furious, water streaming from her long hair.

"You crazy cowboy!" She shouted after the plane that had long since disappeared.

The water was shallow; her feet were touching the rocky bottom. Still grasping the net, she fished the plastic bottle from the lake and waded to shore. Her teeth chattered as she ran down the dock to wrap herself in the towel before unscrewing the bottle cap. She reached two fingers inside and managed to grasp the edge of the sheet of paper. It had been tightly rolled to insert it, but once inside, the paper had unwound into a loose coil. It wouldn't be drawn back through the narrow opening.

Sighing her frustration, Megan collected her things from the dock and went back to the cabin. With a large saw-toothed knife from the utensil drawer, she hacked her way through the thin plastic.

"This had better be good," she grumbled. Water dripped from her hair as she sawed. At last the note was in her hands. The message was neatly scrawled with a black felt pen:

I'll pick you up at 3:00 tomorrow for dinner and dancing. You can get ready at my place. *I have a bathtub!* If you can make it, fly that red bathrobe I saw hanging by your bunk.

                                        Colt

P.S. You owe me one!

"You are a crazy cowboy." She was shaking her head, but her words were murmured with affection.

At three o'clock the following afternoon, Megan stood on the dock, her overnight bag at her feet. The red silk robe was flying from the tall post.

Right on schedule, Colt's plane arrived, the pontoons skimming tracks in the water.

A confident smile dominated his features as he swung onto the dock. "I'm glad to see you could make it." His expression told her he hadn't had any doubts that she would.

"I always pay my debts," she countered smoothly and with a hint of a smile.

He wasted no time bringing down the red robe and helping her board the plane. The lake fell away beneath them as they gained altitude. Megan watched until the cabin disappeared, fighting her conscience for spending an entire afternoon and evening away from the typewriter. She had been blackmailed. No, she had wanted to come. And the promise of a hot soak in a tub had been the clincher. She might as well relax and enjoy it.

"Did you have any trouble getting the bottle out of the water?" Colt asked.

"Oh, no," Megan answered sarcastically. "Unless you would call falling in the lake 'trouble.'"

"You fell in the lake?" He chortled, obviously getting a real kick out of the scenario.

"It wasn't funny," she protested. "It was cold!"

"I guess I should have landed and asked you personally." His tone was a bit more apologetic.

"Why didn't you?" She had wondered about that.

"I was a little rushed, so I thought it would be quicker to drop a note. I've always wanted to sail a note in a bottle. Dropping it from the air was the next best thing." His glance held a trace of dry humor.

"I'm glad you invited me," she confessed. "I was starting to feel trapped—like Sally must be feeling . . ." She trailed off thoughtfully. That observation was new to her. It deserved some consideration. She was never far from her story, constantly gathering research and insight from everything around her.

"Cabin fever."

"What?" She gave herself a mental shake.

"It's called cabin fever. You catch it from being cooped up too long," he informed her.

"This should be good medicine, then," she quipped.

"Um hmm." Colt made an agreeing sound in his throat. "That's what I thought. How's the book coming?"

"Very well. Everything is falling into place," she replied, appreciating his interest and sensing it was genuine.

"If you need any more help be sure to let me know." Behind the gray screen of his glasses, his eyes twinkled with suggestion.

"Thanks." She smiled wryly, aware that her pulse was reacting to his offer even if her mind's answer was a definite "no." "I'll remember that."

It seemed the resort area was popping up before the hour-long flight had really begun. As Colt nosed the plane down to a smooth landing, Megan realized how cut off she had been for the past week. Dock boys scurried to anchor the plane while she and Colt disembarked. There were other people on the dock—other pilots and fishermen. By most standards, it was a peaceful setting, but to Megan it looked like a hub of activity.

Colt carried her bag, depositing it in the back of a fancy black Jeep. He helped her up the high step and they were on their way. About ten minutes down the lake road, they turned onto a wide blacktop drive, braking in front of a rustic log house with a heavy shake roof. In its natural setting of pine trees, it looked perfect.

A stone slab walk led to the double front doors surrounded by more massive stonework. The same masculine boldness carried on into the interior. Stepping across a wide entry hall put them in a living room–den combination. A large stone fireplace claimed a major portion of one wall, flanked on either side by rows and rows of books. Megan nibbled her lower lip, her memory jogging back to that first meeting and the remark she had made about Colt's literary ignorance. It was all too obvious that her assumption had been wrong and unfair. Her recollection of the incident was written all over her face. It hadn't gone unnoticed by her host.

"Not quite a hundred years," he mocked good-naturedly, but with a certain smug satisfaction.

Megan was feeling a little ridiculous. "I guess an apology is in order," she said sheepishly.

"Apology accepted." Long strides put Colt directly in front of the rows of books. He leaned forward, apparently scanning the titles for one in particular. "Here it is," he murmured, drawing it from its place on the shelf. He held it up for display.

Her eyes widened. *"The Realm!"* she breathed in surprise. "You've got my book!" There was always a rush of excitement in seeing her work in the possession of 'real' people. She knew what the sales figures were, but they were so abstract, so impersonal.

"Yes, I've even read it." He continued to mock her with the faulty conclusion that she had drawn about him.

"What did you think?" An enthusiastic glitter lighted her eyes.

He took his time answering, enjoying the nervous anticipation Megan couldn't hide. "You were absolutely right." The pure sensuality in his gaze heightened her nervousness. "You definitely know how to make a person feel something. Whether they want to or not."

And Megan knew he wasn't talking about the book. There was a chemistry between them, that elusive "something" that was either there or it wasn't. She was mesmerized by the silver rings around the black centers of his eyes. They communicated a male interest more clearly than any words could. It was a message Megan wasn't prepared to receive. Her inner reluctance seemed to break the spell holding them silent.

"Let me give you a quick tour of the rest of the house." A fine tension still existed, but they both pretended to ignore it.

"All right," she agreed and followed him through the dining room to the kitchen. Then he showed her the guest bedroom and bath she could use. He seemed to be in a hurry, and Megan noticed that he didn't take off his suede vest even when he stopped to hang up his jacket in the closet. "Are you leaving?" she asked.

"'Fraid so," he confirmed. "I don't want you to think I'm a poor host, but my workday isn't over yet."

"Oh," she murmured. "I hadn't thought about that." She was used to arranging her own schedule and tended to forget that others didn't have the same freedom.

"Just make yourself at home. I'll be back as

soon as I can." He was already on his way out the door.

Except for the rhythmic ticking of the grandfather clock in the hallway, the house seemed to lapse into a lonely silence when Colt left. Megan turned on the stereo to let music fill the emptiness. The tape library indicated more of what she was already finding out. Colt Daniels was a very versatile man. His tastes ran from country to classical, covering the best of everything in between.

The lure of the bathtub was ever present in her mind. With no more reason to wait, she went in and turned the taps wide open, adjusting the temperature on the hot side. She had brought her favorite bubblebath, and she spilled a generous amount in the tub before she slowly sank into the hot, silky water to soak.

It was more than an hour later when Megan emerged from the bathroom in the red silk robe she had flown from the post and a towel wrapped around her wet hair.

Using a hair dryer and curling iron were luxuries she hadn't known the past week. What she had considered necessary bother, she found she was enjoying. Funny how you don't appreciate something until it's gone, she mused.

All that was left to do was slip into her dress when she heard Colt come in the front door.

"Megan, I'm home." His greeting sounded so natural, as if he'd said it a hundred times before.

She tried not to notice the way her heart skipped a beat. "I'll be out in a minute," she called back to him, a disturbed huskiness in her voice.

She slipped the filmy emerald dress over her head and pulled it down around her slim waist. It had a fashionably blousy top and full skirt. The touch of gold from her necklace and earrings set it off just right.

Chapter Four

If Colt had looked handsome as a cowboy, he was devastating in the black tuxedo he was wearing. It set off the width of his shoulders and the ebony sheen of his hair, adding a worldly sophistication without subtracting from his rugged appeal.

"A tux?" Megan was surprised. "I thought this was a small town."

"It's not that small," he corrected with a wry quirk of his mouth. "You don't have to live in L.A. to be civilized."

"Even in L.A. a tuxedo indicates a special occasion." She passed the information along dryly, then tipped her head to one side to ask, "Where are we going?"

"To a business dinner." He didn't seem too anxious to discuss it.

Megan nodded perceptively. "Oh, one of those things you can't get out of, huh?" His disinterested attitude made it a safe guess.

"You could say that." His mouth moved into a faint smile. "I have a feeling I'd be missed if I didn't show up." He glanced at his watch. "Shall we go?"

"I'll get my wrap." She was already moving toward the bedroom.

The sky was dark and dusty with stars when they walked outside. Colt's hand rested lightly on the curve of her waist, guiding her around to the driveway. Instead of the Jeep, a sleek silver Continental was waiting—more proof of his versatility. He drove it with the same easy confidence as he did the Jeep. Somehow both vehicles matched his personality.

The dinner was held in the convention center of a large, elegantly appointed hotel. There were several hundred people already seated when she and Colt were ushered to the head table. "What is this?" Megan whispered. She had been to enough formal award dinners to recognize one when she saw it. And she was uncomfortably aware that the table they were sitting at was generally reserved for the guest of honor. She said as much to Colt.

"I am the guest of honor."

"Why didn't you say so earlier?" Megan demanded in a hissing whisper. Since they were now the center of attention, she smiled and tried to hide her confusion.

"Because it's embarrassing. It's like having your grandmother brag about you to your girlfriend." He slanted her a grin. "But this won't take long and we'll have the rest of the evening." His large hand covered hers to give it a reassuring squeeze.

It helped with her sudden attack of self-consciousness, but she was still a little irritated with him for putting her on the spot. "I hope you realize how lucky you are." The smile was still in place, if a bit tight.

"Lucky?" Dark eyebrows rose in a questioning arch.

"Yes." She nodded. "Lucky that I wore something suited to the occasion. You could have at least warned me that it was going to be formal."

"I said dinner and dancing," he reminded her.

"That could have meant pizza and dancing to a country-western band at the local tavern," she insisted. "I could have shown up in anything—even jeans!"

Someone was speaking from the platform, but Colt's eyes never left her face. A slow smile made a lazy curve on his mouth. "I had faith in you," he murmured. "You've got class, Megan Farraday."

Something inside curled with pleasure at the compliment. It rippled along her nerve ends until every part of her felt touched by it. "It still wasn't fair," she accused, but with no force whatsoever to back it up.

Colt accepted the award for citizen of the year graciously and with his usual charm. He had donated flying services during a freak winter storm and was credited with saving at least three lives.

Megan's eyes moistened with pride when he was given a standing ovation. There was a long line of handshakes and pats on the back, many of them greeting Megan in the same congratulatory manner as they did Colt. Evidently it was just because she was with him. She hadn't done anything to deserve their praise. It was comfortable basking in the overflow of his success, reaping the rewards without the responsibility. Now she understood why so many women lived their lives through their husbands, like her mother. It was comfortable and so much easier. She had seen her mother put away her paintbrushes and close the doors of the struggling storefront art gallery she loved, only to be at her stepfather's side, helping to further his career. He was now an extremely successful businessman.

And Mother still doesn't paint, Megan mused. "That's not for me," she murmured under her breath.

"Megan, I want you to meet a good friend and the best pilot I've got." Colt clamped an affectionate grip on the older man's shoulder. He was skinny and not too tall with kind blue eyes and a winning smile. "Pete Louden," he said by way of simple introduction.

"I'm pleased to meet you, Pete." Megan smiled warmly, returning his brief handshake.

"Where have you been keeping this one?" Pete Louden asked, his assessing gaze sweeping over her in quiet approval.

"This one," Colt mocked, "is Megan Farraday. The young lady in camp twenty-eight."

"Oh . . . the one you have me double-check each day for flags." As soon as the connection was made, he gave Colt a sly wink. "Now I see why."

Megan's gaze flicked to Colt. He arched his eyebrows with a slight shrug of his shoulders. He was guilty.

"I thought Colt told me you were staying out there a month?" Pete continued.

"I am. I just came in for the evening. I'm going back tonight," she assured him, in case he was another one who didn't think she should be out there alone.

The band struck a chord and the crowd paired off, moving onto the dance floor.

"Do you like jazz music?" Colt asked.

"I love it." Her toe was already tapping to the lively beat. It was a fun switch from the usual entertainment provided at such affairs.

"This is supposed to be one of the best jazz bands in the country," he stated. "Think we can do it justice?"

Megan glanced at him through the upward sweep of her lashes. "I don't know about you," she teased, "but I'm willing to give it a shot."

The comment resulted in a contest to see who could "outdance" whom. Their steps became more complicated, effectively challenging the other's skill. But even at that, the ability to function smoothly as a couple was never lost. Out of breath and laughing, they applauded the band when the song ended. It was a relief when the next song had a slower tempo.

Colt's arms stretched out for her in an invitation she didn't even think about resisting. An arm encircled her waist to draw her more fully to him. His natural musky scent blended with the spiciness of his cologne, heightened by the physical exertion of the last dance. After several minutes, Megan realized her heartbeat and breathing still hadn't returned to their normal level. Colt's nearness disturbed her more than she liked to admit.

They danced nearly every dance, stopping only occasionally to get something to drink and take a short breather. Noticing the lateness of the hour, Megan was about to suggest they start back to the camp when Pete Louden walked up.

"Have you noticed the weather?" He directed the question to Colt.

"No, why?" Colt jerked a wary glance at him.

"The fog." Pete shook his head. "It's really souped in. I wouldn't want to be flying in it." He walked on, leaving behind his warning advice.

Colt was frowning when he turned to Megan. "Are you ready to go?"

"Yes." Her expression had lost its humor, too. She was thinking about the hours of work she would miss because of their delay.

Outside, they found that Pete Louden hadn't exaggerated the situation. They couldn't see more than six feet in front of them. It seemed to take forever just to travel the short distance to Colt's house. Megan kept silent so she wouldn't distract him as he cautiously inched the large automobile along the curving lake road through the heavy fog.

"You know you're going to have to stay at my

place?" It had the sound of a question, but it really wasn't. Colt was merely stating the obvious.

With her mind on her work, Megan hadn't even given a thought to where she would sleep tonight. It would be foolish and immature to argue now, when they were more than halfway there. The time for that had been back at the hotel where she could have rented a room. "I know," she said grimly.

"Don't sound so worried," he mocked dryly. "I promise to be a perfect gentleman—all night."

Megan knew he meant it. He was too much of a man to ever force anything if she was unwilling. "I'm not worried about that." She denied his assumption. "But I was having a few regrets about coming tonight."

"Didn't you have a good time?" he asked quickly and sharply.

"I had a wonderful time," she rushed to assure him. "But I had planned to get an early start in the morning. I really don't have a lot of time to spare."

"We'll leave at daybreak if the fog has lifted. You won't lose any time. It's not long till daybreak," he replied, glancing at the lighted clock built into the dashboard.

Megan's eyes were automatically drawn to it also. It was two o'clock. If they flew an hour to the outpost, she wouldn't make it in time to start early anyway. Best thing to do was relax and enjoy the rest of her day off.

Safely back at home, Colt draped an arm

around her waist, walking her along the stone path. At the door, he removed his arm from around her. Instead of finding his key and unlocking the door as Megan expected, he was turning her by the shoulders to face him, slowly bending his head toward her. Automatically her glance went to the strong, smooth line of his mouth coming steadily closer. Anticipation parted her lips a split second before his mouth settled briefly onto hers with natural ease. She felt the fanning warmth of his breath when he withdrew the light pressure of his mouth. It was over almost before it began.

She blinked. "What was that for?"

"A good night kiss." His eyes were smiling.

"You live here." She mockingly reminded him that he wasn't seeing a date to her door.

"I know. I thought you might be more comfortable if I kissed you outside than if I waited until we were alone in my house." A knowing smile crooked his mouth with amusement.

"You crazy cowboy." She laughed, shaking her head at his touching consideration. Unsatisfied with that one, brief taste of him, she let her hands glide up the smooth lapels of his tuxedo to rest on his shoulders.

It seemed to be the invitation Colt was waiting for as an arm curved around her to gather her against him. His hand tunneled under her hair to cup the back of her head and lend his support against the pressure of his kiss as he bent to claim her lips once again.

There was no resemblance to the chaste kiss of

a moment ago. Heat ran fast and strong through her veins under the demanding fire of the hunger she had ignited in him. Her response was just as quick and just as hungry, wanting to give and take at the same time.

Her arms slid around his lean middle, her hands searching out the corded muscles of his back while she arched her spine to get closer. His mouth left hers to graze a trail over her cheek to her ear and on to the sensitive skin of her neck. The moist nuzzling started a whole new chain reaction of sensation. Her pulse was racing wildly. An involuntary sigh trembled through her when he lifted his head.

"We'd better go in the house," she said in a throaty whisper.

"I think we'd better," he echoed, his voice husky.

With one arm remaining around her, he unlocked the door and pushed it open. She pulled back when he urged her forward. There was a question in his smoldering gaze when he looked down at her.

"Let's say good night before we go in." Her voice was still affected by the stimulating encounter.

His look was of shocked disbelief. "You're kidding?" His gaze quickly searched her face, finding it void of any humor. "You're not kidding." He drew in a deep breath, releasing it with a forceful sigh. But the gray eyes with the perpetual twinkle smiled into hers as he lowered his mouth to brush a kiss across her softened lips.

"Good night, Megan," he whispered. The moist heat of his breath was warm on her lips.

"Good night," she answered, reluctant to let it end so soon, but knowing it had to.

Colt kept his word about being a gentleman, as Megan had known he would. She was glad she could trust him because she wasn't too sure of how far she could trust herself anymore. She had sensed a weakness in herself where he was concerned, ever since he kissed her—or rather, she kissed him. She rolled over onto her stomach and crammed the feather pillow under her head, determined not to think about the man in the next room.

The gray streaks of dawn were sweeping across a crisp, clear sky when Megan awakened to a light tapping noise. Someone was knocking on the door. "Yes," she mumbled, sleep hanging heavy in her reply.

"Are you decent?" Colt's muffled voice came through the door.

She took a quick inventory before answering. "I guess so," she said, propping herself against the dark pine headboard, a pillow cushioning her back.

A tray was balanced in one hand while Colt opened the door with the other. The aroma of fresh-brewed coffee came floating across the room, awakening her taste buds even before she could sip the hot, stimulating liquid. Her hand went up to smooth her sleep-rumpled hair in a self-conscious gesture.

"I brought you some coffee and a roll." Colt smiled, setting the small tray on the nightstand next to her.

"Thank you." She smiled back. "That was thoughtful of you."

Colt stood silently studying her while she tasted the coffee.

"I have to confess," he drawled.

"Confess?" She looked up, waiting for him to explain. It was hard to try to second-guess him. She never knew what to expect.

"Yes. I didn't bring you the roll and coffee because I'm a thoughtful person. I used that as an excuse to get into your room."

Megan's eyebrows shot up as her breath lodged in her throat. Her wide-eyed gaze scanned his face to see if he was serious. The freshly shaven features showed no hint of folly, but the twinkle in his eyes belied his story.

"Oh, really," she said evenly, amazed that she could sound so casual. "And why, if I may ask, did you want to get into my room?"

"I wanted to see how you look when you wake up," he baited mischievously.

"Oh, great." It was a dry response, given while she ran her fingers through the disarray of brown-gold tresses.

"I have a bet going with myself," he teased. "I needed to know if you look as good when you wake up in the morning as you do when you go to bed."

"Who won?" She was hesitant to ask.

He narrowed his eyes studiously as if trying to decide. "I did," he said finally.

And Megan realized she knew absolutely nothing about what he'd decided. She laughed and leaned back against the pillow.

"You should do something about those two black streaks down your cheeks and that lipstick smeared all over, though." Lights danced in his eyes. A wide grin split his ruggedly handsome features when her hand darted up to brush her cheek before it registered that he was teasing again.

"You . . . you . . ." she stammered, at a loss for words. Colt was laughing. Curling her fingers into the feather pillow that lay on the bed next to her, she hurled it in one swift motion at his unsuspecting form. "Has anyone ever told you that you're crazy?"

He tried to duck, but he wasn't fast enough. The fluffy pillow landed right in his face. "I think you did." He started to retaliate with the pillow, then tossed it harmlessly back on the bed. "I deserved that," he admitted. "I really came to tell you that we can leave as soon as you're ready. It looks like we'll be having a clear, sunny day.

The serene setting of the outpost camp popped into view and Megan discovered she was over her cabin fever. A night out had been fun and relaxing, but now she was ready to get back to her typewriter. She stole a glance at Colt's strong, smooth profile, so straight and clearly defined. It was one of character. As she watched, an added alertness straightened his spine and a frown of concentration furrowed lines in his forehead.

"Uh oh . . ." A sudden wariness entered his voice.

"What's wrong?" Megan's gaze followed his to the cabin nestled in the trees. At first glance everything appeared to be just the way she had left it. Closer scrutiny, however, revealed a black, gaping hole in one wall of the canvas-topped enclosure. The wall the kitchen was on. Her mind raced. An explosion? A fire? What had caused it?

"It looks like you had a visitor—or *have* a visitor." He made the possible correction.

"What do you mean?" Her eyes were wide, sensing a danger she didn't understand.

"That hole is the work of a bear," he calmly informed her. "I've seen their vandalism before. Unless I miss my guess, the inside is a real mess."

They couldn't get the plane anchored fast enough. Megan helped, but her attention kept straying to the cabin. So did Colt's. Every few seconds they were looking over their shoulders, checking for any movement in the small clearing. But all thoughts of the bear and possible danger fled when a thought struck Megan with sickening force.

"My manuscript!" she breathed. The only copy she had was in the cabin. A dread seized her, churning in the pit of her stomach. Without thought or warning, she started to run, making a beeline for the cabin.

"Hey! Where are you going?" Colt yelled in alarm.

"My manuscript is in there!" A lump caught in her throat when she imagined her work had been destroyed. Her feet flew up the gravel path.

"Don't go in there!" There was the sound of footsteps racing after her. She wasn't listening to his warning.

He caught up with her midway up the winding path. Grabbing her shoulders from behind, he jerked her against his chest, forcing her to stop. "You can't go in there," he stated firmly, turning her in his grasp to face him.

"I have to find it!" she insisted and struggled to break loose.

"Megan!" With a tight grip on her upper arms, he shook her forcefully. "Stop it!"

She looked into the black centers of his eyes, her panic subsiding. His cool rationality was somehow being transmitted to her. Satisfied she was calming down, he released his biting hold. They were both breathing heavily.

"You little fool. You can't just go running in there!" He waved a hand in the direction of the cabin, then returned it to his hip, matching the position of his other hand. He was angry and impatient. The perpetual twinkle was gone from his eyes, replaced by a practical fear Megan knew she had put there. She felt a stab of guilt. "He might still be in here, you know."

She took a deep breath, exhaling slowly. "Well, what should we do?" She decided to rely on his wiser judgment.

"I'll get my rifle out of the plane. You'd better come with me." The last was said as an afterthought. His expression told her he didn't trust her to wait there by herself.

The 30-06 was in Colt's hands and loaded in record time. "You wait here while I check out the cabin," he instructed.

"I'm going with you," she stated.

He must have known she would refuse because he didn't try to reason with her. "Stay behind me," he ordered gruffly.

They didn't talk on the way to the cabin. Megan's nerves were jumping with every tiny sound: the whisper of the wind through the trees, a rustle somewhere off in the brush—it all worked on her imagination and sent adrenaline pumping through her system. Colt used the rifle barrel to cautiously nudge the door open. The squeak of its hinges grated her nerves to a raw edge.

Colt's rifle was loaded and ready, his finger poised on the trigger. There was the coiled tension of a predatory beast about him when he entered the cabin. Megan followed a step behind. Two loud sighs of relief sounded simultaneously as the silent cabin attested to its emptiness.

The bear was gone, but a mass of destruction was left in its wake. The refrigerator was lying face down, with litter and canned goods from the cupboards and shelves strewn all around it. Except for the hole ripped in the canvas, the structure itself was intact.

With no threat of danger remaining, Megan's thoughts flashed back to her work. She rushed to the table. The typewriter appeared to be untouched, but the papers she had stacked beside it were scattered. She had slipped the manuscript itself in its unfinished form inside her leather portfolio before she left. It wasn't on the table where she had left it. The sensation of panic rose again, constricting her throat muscles as she looked around. A quick glance under the table divulged its whereabouts. It was shoved back against the wall, unopened and unharmed. Relief weakened her limbs as it flooded over her.

They began to clean up. Together they uprighted the cumbersome refrigerator, and Colt relit its pilot. The rest had looked bad, but it didn't take long to put everything back in order.

"I'll have to go in and get a piece of canvas to patch this hole," Colt remarked as he surveyed the damaged wall. "Why don't you put a few things in a suitcase and come with me? You can stay at my house for a couple of days."

"How do you know he'll be gone in a couple of days?" she wondered.

"I don't." He admitted. "That's why I'm going to stay here and wait for him."

"If you're staying, there's no reason for me to leave," she reasoned. "I'm sure I'll be safe with you here." How could he argue? He gave her a measuring look but didn't try to persuade her further.

He did insist that she accompany him when he flew back to the resort to get the patching materials for the tent. She didn't resist. Spending the afternoon alone with a bear wasn't on her list of things to experience.

"I can't figure out what made the bear break in." Colt shook his head, a frown creasing his forehead. "Are you positive there wasn't any food out—scraps in the garbage, fruit or something?"

Searching her brain for a clue, Megan slowly shook her head in a negative answer. "I can't think of anything . . . the apples!" She suddenly remembered. "I left the apples out!" she exclaimed. "Oh, I can't believe I did that." Her tone was distressed. "I've been so careful—and then to walk off and leave a bowl of apples sitting on the table . . ." She moaned.

"Don't be too hard on yourself. It was one in a million chances that *one* bowl of apples left out for *one* night would happen to get the attention of a bear." Colt offered consolation.

"I guess I'm just lucky," she responded dryly.

"Lucky you weren't in that cabin," he reminded her.

"Why do you suppose the bear came while I was gone?" A puzzled, thoughtful look pinched her face. "I had the bowl of apples sitting out all night the nights I was up working late."

"The smoke from your fire might have kept him away," he speculated with a shrug.

"Then all we have to do is build a fire." It seemed a simple solution.

"I doubt if that would be enough to stop him now. He knows there's food inside. It's likely he'll come back looking for more." Obviously Colt didn't want to oversimplify a potentially dangerous situation. "We'll bait him tonight and see what happens."

"What will we use for bait?" Megan's interest was sparked by the new adventure.

"We know he likes apples. We'll give some more of them to him."

"He ate the last of them. If you want to use apples we'll have to get more," she informed him.

"We can pick some up while we're in town." He had everything under control. She liked his air of confidence. It stopped short of arrogance just in time to be attractive.

In town they bought all the things they needed, including a hunting license for Megan. That was Colt's idea. Since they planned to shoot the bear, he suggested she buy a license. He didn't have to twist her arm. She was already formulating in her mind how she could incorporate this experience into her book. Loading the mending supplies and a bushel of red apples onto the yellow floatplane, they headed for camp number twenty-eight for the second time that day.

Megan worked the rest of the afternoon and Colt walked the small island in search of the bear. At one point, the island was only a stone's throw across the channel. He could have gone back already and forgotten about the taste of food he'd had. Only time would tell. It was nerve-wracking to have to wonder.

The glowing orange ball was fast sinking deep in the western sky when Megan snapped her portfolio shut on another chapter. Spotting Colt standing on the dock, she ambled down the path to join him. Leaning a shoulder against the tall post, he appeared to be engrossed in the picturesque sunset. Wisps of dark hair swept down across his forehead, adding to his rakish appeal. His arms were crossed on the plaid flannel shirt stretched tightly over his hard-muscled chest. New Levis covered the tops of the leather western boots, his legs casually crossed at the ankles. That same silent power and latent sexuality prevailed, dressed as he was or in a tuxedo. It didn't matter.

"Hi." Colt grinned, his voice low.

"Hi." She smiled back at him.

"Come here. I'll buy you a ticket to the best show in town." Still leaning against the post, he stretched his arms toward Megan, inviting her to stand next to him. When he adjusted his position slightly to accommodate her in the curve of his arm, she leaned comfortably into his side, the light pressure of his hold keeping her close. They stood that way for long minutes, watching the sun literally disappear, only its lingering rays of light shooting up above the horizon.

Unconsciously a wistful sigh escaped from somewhere deep within her, a sigh of sadness that it had ended. The beauty had faded away. It seemed almost a spiritual experience, one they had shared. A squeeze on Megan's shoulder indicated he felt it, too.

He brushed his lips across her hair, breathing in the sweet fragrance of her perfume. She knew if she looked at him he would kiss her. Her heart skipped a beat. She raised her lips slowly, a slight upward tilt to her chin. Through the veiling sweep of her lashes, her gaze traveled past the tanned column of his throat to stop at the sensuous line of his mouth, flanked by those attractive lines, and finally moved on to meet his intense dark eyes. His hand glided across her shoulder, his fingertips tracing the cord of her neck and burrowing into her hair, tightening into the toffee-gold thickness.

He gently tugged her head back so he could find her lips. Her heart was hammering against her ribs as he bent to close the distance between them. His mouth sought hers, gently tasting, gently probing. Colt shifted so that his back was against the post, turning Megan more fully to him. She slid her hands around him to familiarize herself again with the feel of him.

The breeze felt cool on her love-warmed face when Colt broke the kiss. Only a couple of inches separated their lips.

"You could work up a man's appetite." Colt's voice was low and husky between his frequent, brief kisses on her cheek, her temple, her hair.

"It's dinner time. No wonder you're hungry." She feigned naiveté.

"I'm hungry as a bear," he growled, transferring his kisses to a point below her ear, nibbling and nuzzling the sensitive skin.

"Come on." Her laugh was breathless as she twisted easily from his hold. "I'll get you an apple."

Chapter Five

Colt hadn't fixed the black gaping wound in the canvas. First, they were going to use the hole to observe the edge of the clearing a number of yards from the cabin where they had dumped a small pile of apples to bait the bear.

Two of the straight-backed wooden chairs were drawn up to face the hole, where they had a good view of the trap. Colt's 30-06 and the 30-30 he had left with Megan were standing against the board wall, loaded and ready, within easy reach. A fire burned in the stove for warmth, but they had extinguished the lights of the lanterns.

Megan was taut with expectation. The thought of a bear suddenly bursting into the clearing kept her coiled, ready to spring into action. She practiced, in her mind, what she would do when she saw him. She imagined herself calmly rising to her feet, taking careful aim, waiting for just the right moment and then shooting. There was no margin for error.

Colt was reposed, balancing the chair on its two hind legs. "You might as well relax," he advised. "This could take all night."

It was easier said than done. But as the minutes stretched into hours, Megan's tense anticipation began to wane. She pulled her jacket more tightly around her, a shield from the chilly north-country air. The star-studded heaven consoled her with its familiarity. This was the same Big Dipper, the same Milky Way she had seen as a child. The same one her friends could see in Los Angeles, if they would only look. The world wasn't so big after all, and the wilderness of Rainy Lake, Ontario, wasn't really so remote. It was a nice place to be.

"A penny for your thoughts." Colt broke her reverie.

Smiling, she shook her head. "I wouldn't want you to feel cheated."

"You seemed to be far away. Were you thinking of home . . . of Los Angeles?" he pressed.

Her shoulders lifted in a slight shrug. "Sort of."

"Are you missing your . . . friends?" He hesitated on the last word.

"No." She glanced at his face, nearly hidden by the shadows. "I haven't really given them much thought."

"Is there someone special you should be missing?" His question sounded strained.

Her smile was masked by the darkness. Now

she understood all the questions. "There's no one special," she replied.

"Except Nick," he reminded her, the tautness erased from his voice, his usual sense of humor at work.

"Except Nick," she agreed with a smile.

"How about you? Is there a Sally stuck away in a closet somewhere?" It was suddenly important that she know.

"No, there are no ghosts in my closet." After a moment of silence, he added. "The only Sally in my life was exorcised a long time ago." There was no trace of bitterness; it was merely a statement. But he must have loved her once or he wouldn't have referred to her as Sally.

"I'm sorry," she sympathized.

"I'm not," he countered. "We would never have been happy. She wanted me to sell out and move to New York and I wanted her to stay here with me. We just weren't meant for each other."

It was a classic example of exactly what Megan feared would happen to her if she allowed herself to fall in love, the difference being that she might not have the willpower to walk away.

"I guess she felt her career was important, too." Megan tried to present another point of view—her point of view.

"I'm sure you're right or she would be here," he conceded. "Only her career was being a social butterfly. Her family was of the elite—very wealthy. She wanted me to escort her to all the endless affairs and parties." He sighed. "I didn't think I'd fit in."

Megan was inclined to agree. He was a man in every sense of the word. He was made to protect and provide for his woman, never to be a reflection of her, an ornament. That's exactly what she couldn't—she wouldn't—let happen to her. She didn't want to be an ornament on some man's arm either or just a reflection of his successes. There seemed to be no way to compromise. That's why she had to keep reminding herself to be careful. Since she had met Colt, she hadn't been doing a very good job of it. She would have to do better, she chided herself.

"Haven't you had any close calls? No wedding bells ringing in your ears?"

"No." Her answer was emphatic. "I never let anything get that serious."

Even in the dark, she could see the question in his eyes. "What are you afraid of?" There was no mockery in his query.

"I'm not 'afraid' of anything," was her too-quick comeback.

His silence begged for an explanation.

She felt forced to comply. "I don't think I would make a husband very happy—or maybe he wouldn't make me happy." Perhaps that was closer to the truth.

"Could you run that by me again?" He requested.

"In case you haven't noticed, I like my work. It is very important to me." A defensiveness crept into her voice because a lot of people considered her attitude to be selfish.

"I noticed," he cut in.

"Anyway," she continued, "to be a writer is all I've ever wanted. Now I'm there. I am a successful writer. But, if I'm to stay there, at the top of the proverbial ladder, then I must work. And work means time. That time isn't always when it's most convenient. Sometimes, it's all night long. There are deadlines to meet, and many times the dinner won't be waiting on the table or the slippers waiting by the fire." She looked at him through the darkness. "With me, it's breakfast at midnight and steak at ten in the morning. Now do you understand?"

"I understand what you're saying, but I think you're wrong." He continued before she could protest. "You're saying you don't fit the stereotyped version of a wife. A lot of men don't fit the stereotyped version of a husband, either."

"I think—" She tried to cut in, but he wasn't finished.

"If you think you're intelligent and open-minded enough to allow a man to pursue a career or hobby, or whatever, why are you so quick to assume that a man couldn't be just as understanding, even encouraging?" It sounded different when he said it like that. "We're not all biased chauvinists," he mocked.

Truth rang loudly in his words, but experience was a better teacher. "I can't dispute what you say, in theory. But in practice I haven't found it to be so."

"How would you know? You said you've never gotten that close to anyone," he reminded her.

She hesitated briefly, deciding how far she

wanted to go with this discussion. It seemed a little late to turn back now. "But I can see," she chided. "My mother is a good artist—maybe even great, we'll never know. She is what you would call an ornament, merely a reflection of my stepfather. She performs her wifely duties well, but there's nothing left for her."

"I'm sorry for her if that's the case," Colt offered. "But maybe she wants it that way."

"Why would she want it that way?" Megan frowned.

"Someone wiser than I once said, 'Show me someone who has never failed, and I'll show you someone who has never tried.' Every time you sit at your typewriter, you're taking a risk. You're risking rejection. For some, the risk is too great, the price is too high, so they choose a safer route. We weren't all born with an adventurous spirit." There was an irrefutable logic in the words he spoke.

It was hard for Megan to admit to herself the possibilities of his suppositions. She'd been thinking the way she had for so long it would take some serious consideration before she could change. If she even wanted to.

"I'm glad you're an adventurous woman." Colt steered the conversation in a lighter direction.

"Why?" Megan was curious.

"If you weren't, you wouldn't be here and I would never have met you," he replied, that twinkle again in his eyes.

"And you would have been spared a lot of trouble," she reminded him. "You would be home in a nice soft bed instead of sitting on these hard chairs, looking through a hole in the wall, freezing to death." She groaned as she shifted for a more comfortable position on the hard seat.

"Look at the cynic!" he mocked. "What happened to the enthusiastic bear hunter?" His reach spanned the short distance between them. Taking her hand in his, he squeezed it affectionately. "Besides, if I was home in my nice soft bed, I would be alone. I would much rather be miserable here with you."

The early morning hours came and still no bear. Megan was nodding in her chair as sleep threatened to overtake her.

"Why don't you go to bed and get some sleep?" Colt urged. "I'll wake you if anything happens."

He didn't have to say it a second time. Megan was already on her way to the bunk.

The night passed with no sign of the bear. Megan dug out the bacon and eggs to try her hand at fixing Colt some breakfast. Cooking was not one of her best suits, but she could get along.

Her hair hung soft and full around the shoulders of the red robe, swinging gently as she moved about, setting the table and spreading the fat pieces of bacon in the bottom of a heavy iron skillet. The coffee was done and the eggs were waiting in a bowl to be scrambled.

"Mmm, that smells good." Colt inhaled the mouth-watering aromas while he closed the cabin door. He brought with him the towel and the soap he had taken to the lake.

Megan smiled over her shoulder. She heard his

footsteps coming up behind her while she was busy at the stove. His hand under her hair, fitting itself lightly to the curve of the back of her neck. Leaning his head over her shoulder, his cheek was almost parallel to hers. Megan turned to look at him, as he knew she would. He was waiting for it. He lowered his mouth onto her lips, moving over them slowly and pervasively. The kiss started a curling heat spreading through her. She was conscious of the faint scrape of the stubble beard on his chin, but she didn't mind.

Megan suddenly broke off the kiss. "The bacon's burning!" she cried. Colt was way ahead of her. With one swift movement, he turned off the stove and picked up the spatula. Fishing the charred strips out of the smoking grease, he laid them on the layers of paper towels Megan had reserved for them. "Oh, it's ruined!" she moaned. "I'll fix you some more." She reached for the opened package beside her.

"Hey, wait a minute!" Colt took the package from her, studying its contents. "I remember hearing somewhere that bacon is good bear bait. Let's save it and try it tonight."

"That's fine with me," Megan agreed. "I'd probably just burn it again anyway."

"And I'd help." He smiled mischievously, pecking a kiss on her unsuspecting lips.

The meatless breakfast tasted good just the same. Colt didn't complain. Sitting across the table from him was becoming a habit Megan hated to break. He was good company and good looking—a rare combination. The shadowy growth of a night's beard enhanced his ruggedness. An easy strength was in his masculine features.

"I have to go check out some of the other camps today. Do you want to come along?" Colt raised his coffee cup to his lips, his eyes watching her inquiringly.

"How long will you be gone?" She didn't want to lose a whole day.

"A couple of hours," he informed her. "I won't be leaving until this afternoon. I want to catch a few hours' sleep. Tonight is liable to be another long one." He didn't look tired, so Megan had forgotten that he hadn't slept all night.

"Do you think he'll come tonight?" Megan was dubious.

"I don't know." He rubbed his tired eyes. "I'm beginning to think he's left the island."

"How will we know if he has?" she asked.

"We won't. You won't be able to stay here at night." He answered what was really on her mind.

She nodded her understanding. With the real danger of a bear lurking somewhere in the woods, she wasn't arguing. She might be headstrong, but she wasn't stupid.

While Colt slept, Megan typed.

She was pleased with the progress she was making. The writing was coming easily, which gave the story the smooth, natural flow she was striving for. By lunch time she was ready for a break.

Colt wanted her to wake him around noon. She

walked over to where he lay sleeping and gently nudged his shoulder. He didn't look vulnerable even when he was asleep. He appeared strong and dominant in spite of his passive state. She had to nudge him twice more to wake him from the deep slumber. Thick, black, spiky lashes slowly opened from the slate-gray eyes. A slow lazy smile curved his lips. "It's nice waking up to you." His voice was low and sluggish. "It keeps me from rolling over and going back to sleep." She brushed off his suggestion of a compliment, but it warmed her inside.

"I was just going to fix some lunch." Megan moved toward the wall that was the kitchen. "Do you want some?"

"Sure." He sat up on the edge of the low bunk. "I could use a shave," he declared, rubbing a hand over the scratchy stubble on his chin.

"I've got a razor you can use," Megan offered. "And there's some warm water in the tea kettle on the stove." She got him a new toothbrush and disposable razor out of the blue overnight bag, then returned to prepare lunch. "Is ham okay?" she asked.

"Ham's fine," Colt answered. He was finished shaving by the time Megan had their sandwiches made and on the table, along with potato chips and pickles.

The direction they took when they left the camp this time was different. The only route Megan had taken before was to the resort and back, so she was surveying the new scenery with interest. Basically, it was a repeat of what she had already seen: masses of fall-colored trees around glassy waterways that mirrored the autumn splendor.

Seemingly from out of nowhere, a rich green meadow was spread below them, an oasis in an endless desert of trees. The unusual setting prompted Megan to utter the comment, "Look, land!" She chuckled to herself, thinking she sounded like Christopher Columbus.

Colt's smile was one of amusement. "That's Moose Meadows, one of my favorite places," he confided. "Sometimes I take a boat from one of the camps and spend the day fishing. It's also a good place to hunt moose. That's why it's called Moose Meadows." He affirmed the obvious.

"I love it!" Megan responded with her natural exuberance. "It's so pretty! I'd like to try fishing there sometime. How far is it from my camp?"

"Oh, I'd say about three miles, by water. It's easy to find. Just keep bearing to the right after you cross the channel and you'll run right into it."

While he answered her question, he was setting the small yellow plane down at another of the outpost camps. There was evidence that it was being occupied, but the boat was gone and no one was in sight.

"They must be out fishing," Colt reasoned. Megan waited in the plane when he walked up to check the cabin. On his way back he stopped before walking onto the dock and pulled out three good boards that were stored beneath it. Stacking them to easier accommodate his grasp, he carried them to the plane and slid them inside.

"What are the boards for?" Megan asked curiously when they were once again in the air.

"I'm going to build a tree stand, farther away from the cabin, and see if we have any better luck tonight," he answered.

They stopped at four more camps. Each time Colt took the boards that were stored under the individual docks for repair purposes.

Two and a half hours had sped by when they arrived back at their own camp. Megan helped Colt carry the heavy lumber to the spot he had chosen for the tree stand. With hammer and nails he always carried in the plane, in no time at all they had a suitable tree stand—or "treehouse" as Megan mistakenly, but continually, called it.

Megan's excitement for the bear trap was returning as Colt's new plan began to take shape.

Trying to fit in a couple of hours of work before dusk, she had a hard time concentrating on her story. Colt took that time to mend the hole in the canvas wall that the bear had ripped open.

With dinner over and a fresh thermos of coffee tucked under Colt's arm, they set out for the tree stand. Megan carried two blankets folded across her arms and the lantern, while Colt brought the rifles. The bacon had been hung from a tree at the edge of the small clearing earlier. The apples had been squashed to release a stronger odor. Colt helped Megan climb up the branches of the tree to the wooden platform they had built. After handing the rifles up to her, he hoisted himself up smoothly and effortlessly.

It was dark and a bit on the cold side. They

wrapped blankets around themselves, Indian style, before sitting down against the trunk of the tree. Colt positioned the rifles next to him and turned out the lantern. As their eyes made the adjustment, the night didn't appear so dark. When Megan strained her eyes to search the shadows she could make out the mound of apples in the center of the clearing. She was having no trouble at all smelling them.

As had happened the night before, midnight came and went and still no bear. Megan was feeling the cold in spite of the blanket she was wearing. The necessity of their sedentary position didn't allow for any added circulation. Colt felt her shiver next to him. "Do you want some coffee to warm you up?" His tone was hushed, almost a whisper.

"Yes, I think I'd better. I'm starting to get chilled clear through." Her teeth chattered.

Colt passed her the handleless cup of hot coffee. She wrapped both hands around it for its heat to penetrate her fingers. Swallowing a big gulp, she let it slide down to her stomach, warming her from the inside out.

"Come here and get warm," Colt ordered. He opened his blanket for her to slide in beside him.

She snuggled up to him, balancing her coffee so she wouldn't spill it. The added warmth of the extra blanket and Colt's arm around her shoulder brought instant relief from the cold.

"Aren't you cold?" she queried.

"Not anymore." The suggestion in his remark made Megan more conscious of his nearness than she wanted to admit. She had vowed to keep their relationship light and she didn't like the way she was feeling. She didn't want to notice the hard band of muscles that flexed in his chest when he shifted for a more comfortable position, or the steamy breath, escaping the provocative mouth that was such a potent force.

"Would you like some coffee?" She offered him a drink from her cup.

"Thanks, I thought you'd never ask." He took two big gulps before handing it back to her.

"I've had enough. You can keep it." She waved the cup away. He added more from the thermos and sipped it while they waited.

"Look at that!" Colt squeezed her shoulder to get her attention. She saw some movement at the apple pile.

"What is it?" she whispered.

"It's a raccoon." After he told her, she could make out the image of the furry critter.

"He's going to eat all the apples!"

"He'll get a bellyache before he could eat that many apples," he countered with amusement.

"It looks like he brought along a guest," she whispered, pointing to another one.

"Those little bandits!" he hissed. "If there are any more, I'll have to run them off."

No more came, so they watched the two prowl around and walk through the mushy apple heap.

"I hope we didn't go to all this trouble just for those little rascals." Colt sighed. "But it's beginning to look that way," he conceded.

"What time is it?" Megan yawned; she was beginning to tire.

Colt pushed the illumination button on his watch. "Oh, it's only one o'clock. There's still plenty of time for Mr. Bear to show," he said.

Apparently their voices scared off the raccoons; they went scampering into the cover of the woods.

Megan saw a large, dark shadow in her peripheral vision looming at the edge of the clearing, moving unhurriedly toward them. Now she knew why the raccoons ran. Her fingers clutched at the front of Colt's vest. "Colt." The barely audible whisper almost stuck in her throat.

"I see it!" he breathed. His body was suddenly tense and alert, all his senses tuned to the danger.

He cautiously handed Megan the 30-06, the more powerful of the two rifles. When she had a good hold, Colt reached over and flipped off the safety. He moved in behind her so that her back was supported against part of his chest, to help absorb the impact of the recoil. He watched across her shoulder.

"Don't get in a hurry." He whispered the instructions in her ear. "Wait until he goes for the apples." Megan's heart was hammering so loudly she was afraid the bear might hear.

Raising the weapon to her shoulder, she took careful, deliberate aim. She followed the animal's every move through the sights that were mounted on the rifle.

After consuming the bacon, the bear moved on to the apples. He was eating them, but he had his hindquarters turned in their direction.

"Wait until he turns around." Colt continued to talk her through the paces. At that moment, the massive creature turned, almost as if he could hear them talking.

"Not yet." Colt literally breathed the words. "When he stands up, aim at his chest and shoot."

Colt whistled. The bear stood still, listening. "Get ready!" he warned. He whistled again, loud and shrill.

The bear stood up on his hind legs, his head swaying back and forth. Megan had him dead center in the sights.

"Now!" Colt urged. She was aware of all that was taking place, but it seemed like it was happening to someone else. She was just an observer. She froze! "Shoot, Megan!" Colt wasn't trying to be quiet anymore. The bear had spotted them and began to move toward them. Any second he would be on all fours. Her perfect shot would be lost and the bear would be on top of them. She squeezed the trigger—again and again until there was no more noise.

Colt took the empty gun from her hands. "How many times do you want to shoot him?" Colt laughed.

"Did I get him?" Megan was trembling.

"The first shot! Didn't you see him go down? That was a close call!" Colt was talking fast, a little shaken himself.

"I didn't see anything. I had my eyes closed," she told him.

"A bear was coming for you and you closed your eyes?" He was incredulous.

"That's why I closed my eyes. I was so scared when he started to come at us that I froze! So I closed my eyes and pretended I was shooting at a paper target." Megan made a flimsy attempt at explaining. She wasn't making much sense to Colt, judging from his expression of utter disbelief.

"It was a closer call than I realized." He heaved a sigh of relief.

After helping Megan carry the rifles, blankets and thermos to the cabin, Colt took some towels and his hunting knife with him back to the clearing to dress out the bear. Megan was glad he refused her offer of assistance. She had found out she didn't have the stomach for shooting an animal, even in self-defense. The prospect of cleaning one was far less appealing.

She sat down at the typewriter, intending to work while waiting for Colt to return, but as the excitement of the hunt wore off she became increasingly drowsy. The bunk was so inviting that she finally gave up and lay down. That was the last she knew until the noise of Colt entering the cabin roused her. He walked over and stood next to her bunk, the fresh smell of outdoors following him.

"Are you awake?" he asked softly. The graying light of dawn from the window behind him cast his image into sharp relief.

"Yes," she mumbled, half in, half out of sleep. "Is it time to get up or are you just going to bed?" she continued thickly.

"Neither. I'm going to take the meat on into

town before the sun gets to it and spoils it. I'll see you tomorrow."

"Okay." She forced a tired response.

"Go back to sleep." It was the last thing she heard. She didn't catch the glitter of amusement in Colt's silver-dark eyes when he affectionately reached down and tousled her head before he left.

Chapter Six

The Indian summer held for yet another day. Megan's airy yellow blouse and white shorts were indicative of the unseasonably warm weather. The sun's rays on the canvas roof heated the room to an almost uncomfortable level. Megan had the door ajar for ventilation. She had stayed at her typewriter all morning, resisting the beckon of the sunny dock overlooking a shimmering blue-green lake of glass. She wanted to get as much writing done as possible before Colt came. He hadn't given her any indication as to what time he would be there.

Her expectant glance kept darting to the window every few minutes. She felt irritated. Usually she couldn't get her attention away from her book. Today she couldn't get her attention on it. She felt vaguely unsettled knowing that Colt

Daniels could prevail in her thoughts, unbidden. He was getting in the way of her writing and it bothered her.

With a loud sigh, she pushed away from the table. "No point in struggling," she muttered to herself. She walked to the refrigerator and fixed an icy glass of mineral water. It was time for a break. Succumbing to the spring-fever feeling she was at war with, she took her drink and meandered toward the dock.

Her senses immediately picked out the faint humming sound of an airplane from the normal woodsy noises. Her pulse accelerated, but she deliberately slowed her footsteps so it wouldn't look as if she'd been standing around waiting for him.

Colt was vaulting onto the dock at about the same time Megan reached it. He was wearing a pale blue tee-shirt and an old pair of jeans faded and worn soft to hug his hips and thighs.

"I'm glad to see you're ready to go." He grinned, a stray lock of hair falling across his forehead.

The greeting momentarily threw her. "Ready to go where?" she asked warily.

"Oh, didn't I tell you?" Colt blamed it on innocent oversight. "I'm taking you fishing."

"No, you didn't tell me," she countered. Not that it would have made any difference. "I can't take the whole afternoon and go fishing," she insisted. "I have to work sometime."

Obviously the announcement didn't deter him.

She watched him reach into the plane to retrieve two fishing poles and a tackle box.

"We're going to have a picnic, too," he calmly informed her as he set out a woven wood picnic basket and a blanket.

"Aren't you listening? I said I have to work." Megan was irritated at the way he was brushing that fact aside, as if it were an unimportant detail.

He stopped unloading and turned to look at her. "You have to stop to eat," he argued complacently. "If we take too long, you can work later this evening."

It made sense, Megan admitted silently. Especially since the beautiful weather had contributed to her inability to concentrate. She would probably get more done after the sun went down anyway.

Colt sensed her hesitation. "We're going to Moose Meadows." He dangled one more carrot in front of her nose and watched her with a lazy grin that seemed to say he knew she would change her mind.

Megan remembered the gorgeous meadow she had seen from the air and knew she wasn't going to say no to the chance to explore it on foot. Her shoulders lifted in a shrug of surrender. "You talked me into it." And she was aware that it hadn't taken any arm-twisting.

After they had loaded all the fishing paraphernalia into the boat, Megan picked her way to the front. Colt assisted her with a steadying hand as she tried to avoid stepping on the assorted clutter.

He tossed her a red flotation cushion to soften the hard bench seat.

The small outboard motor made enough racket to discourage any lengthy conversation as it pushed them slowly across the lake. They had gone about a mile when they passed another camp. They waved at the two men standing on the dock. In return, one of the men held up a stringer of fish, boasting of the day's catch.

"I hope we have such good luck," Megan shouted above the noisy motor.

"We will." Colt's answer was confident. As they neared their destination, he watched the shoreline, looking for the best place to beach the boat. There was the scrape of aluminum against the rocky lake bottom and Colt cut the motor. It seemed unnaturally quiet and still after the constant high-pitched whine.

The boat rocked with the shifting of weight as Colt moved toward the front. Megan slid to one side of the bench so he could climb over and make the jump to shore. Then he was dragging the boat until it was securely banked and helping Megan step over the edge.

Up a slight rise from the lake was a beautiful green meadow—Moose Meadows. It was surrounded completely by trees leafed out in every autumn hue. A tiny place amid the forest for the animals to graze by night and bed down in the warmth of the sun by day, it was fresh and untouched, as was all this wilderness land. Megan was awed by its creation.

"Do you think we can find a suitable spot for a

picnic?" Teasing lights danced in Colt's eyes as he asked.

"I think so." Megan laughed, because any place in the meadow would be perfect. It was flat and soft with a thick cushion of green grass.

"How about right here?" A hand gesture indicated the place where they were standing.

"It's fine." She approved his choice, then helped to spread out the large blanket. Colt set the picnic basket down in the center.

"Are you hungry yet? Or would you rather fish?" He made it her choice.

"Let's fish," Megan decided, remembering the full stringer they'd seen earlier.

He grabbed her hand and gave her a gentle tug. "Let's go." They ran the distance down the slope, past the trees, to the edge of the lake.

The first step to fishing was casting out the line, which was not quite so simple as Megan had thought it would be. When Colt did it, it looked easy. But when she tried, it ended up in the stand of trees behind them. Colt laughed at her feeble attempts, but he patiently instructed her until she could manage on her own. By the seventh or eighth attempt, she was smiling and feeling rather proud of herself.

But casting the bait into deep water wasn't the only frustrating part of fishing, Megan found out when the waiting began. They sat in silence on a fallen tree trunk near the water's edge, waiting for something to strike.

She was asking herself what the big attraction was for all those fishermen when her pole bent almost double, then started jerking up and down. Hanging on tightly, she tried to turn the crank on the reel, but she could barely move it. "Colt!" she yelled. "I think I've got something!" He was already beside her.

"Loosen your drag." Since she had no idea what he was talking about, he reached over and twisted the screw on the reel. It was all she could do to hang onto the pole. The line went whizzing out from the reel.

"He's getting away!" She was frantically trying to hold onto the rod and turn the reel. She wasn't doing a very good job of either.

Colt was laughing at her predicament. "He's not getting away, he's just going for a little swim. Look at him break water! He's a beauty!"

She saw it jump from the water, glistening silver in the sunlight. She found it incredible that the big fish so far out from shore was actually on the end of her line.

"Start bringing him in." Colt talked her through the paces. "Don't get in a hurry. Let him run, then bring him in again. You've got to play him in. He's too big to horse him in. He'll break your line."

Megan followed Colt's expert advice and played the fish for a long twenty minutes. He finally tired and she reeled him in, landing him on the bank beside her. Megan was quivering from the excitement. Now she knew why all those fishermen kept trying.

"Talk about beginner's luck! That's a lunker!" Colt was examining and admiring her catch.

"I thought you said we were fishing for lake trout?" Megan looked at him curiously, frowning when he threw back his head to laugh.

"It is a lake trout. It's also a lunker—as in *big*." He demonstrated, holding his hands apart in a three-foot span. "It'll probably go eight or ten pounds."

"Oh." The information didn't mean very much to her since she had no past experience to compare with.

"Would you like to have this mounted?" Colt inquired. "You'll have a bearskin rug to show for your trip, so you might as well have your trout mounted, too. Most of the guys that come out here would give their eyeteeth for either one of them."

"Since it's my first fish, I guess I should have it mounted," Megan agreed.

"I don't think you have any idea what you've got here." Colt shook his head back and forth. "Years go by without ever seeing a fish that would come close to this one."

"Really?" She looked again at the huge fish, seeing it with new appreciation. This was a trophy fish—a lunker! And on her first try! "I guess I just didn't realize what I'd caught." She laughed in apology.

"I guess you didn't," he agreed. "You've heard all the jokes about the one that got away?"

Megan nodded in recognition of the famous fisherman's line. "Who hasn't?"

"Well, this is the one." Colt's glance flicked briefly to the trout before it came back to her face. "He's done a lot of nibbling on a lot of different hooks, but for some reason you were the only one who could catch him. I wonder why that is."

Something in the probing gray of his eyes changed the mood from playful to serious, all in a single second and all without a change in expression or tone of voice. She knew what he was really saying. He could be caught. But Megan wasn't sure of that kind of fishing.

"It's hard to say," she murmured in answer to his question.

Then Colt was flashing that crooked grin and Megan wondered if she had imagined a hidden meaning in his earlier statement. Either way, the mood was instantly lighter and she was glad.

He put the trout on a metal stringer and left it in the cold water for the time being. "Are you tired of fishing?" Amusement gleamed in his eyes.

"Tired?" she scoffed. "We just got started." She began to bait her hook, anxious to get it back in the water. She'd been bitten by the fishing bug. Now she was one of "those fishermen," too.

Two hours later, Megan dropped down beside Colt on the blanket. Thick tufts of meadow grass beneath made the blanket lumpy but soft.

"Now that I think about it, I'm starving," she remarked, mildly surprised to find that out.

"I've been trying to feed you for the past hour," Colt reminded her as he began removing an assortment of containers from the basket.

"I know. I know," she admitted. "I got carried away. It seems to be a trait of mine." She helped take out the paper plates and plastic utensils.

"Either that or you're hooked," he observed. "Getting you out of that fishing hole was like pulling teeth!" A hint of humor deepened the slashes at the corners of his mouth. "And after I slaved in the kitchen all morning preparing this fine meal." The despairing shake of his head mocked her while he peeled the lid off the bucket of fried chicken he had bought at a fast food restaurant.

He handed Megan a paper cup. "And for your pleasure, *Mademoiselle*, the finest from France." With a fake French accent and a flourish of his hand, Colt produced a bottle wrapped in a white towel. He twisted off the cap and poured the bubbly clear liquid into her glass.

"Is that . . . ?" She trailed off, because she wasn't sure. It could have been sparkling wine.

"Yes, *Mademoiselle* . . . mineral water." There was another flourish as he displayed the bottle and again that silly, attractive mixture of a drawl and a French accent.

"You're incredible." She laughed, sipping at the effervescent drink. "It's cold." She was surprised.

"That's because it's been in the freezer most of the morning." The accent was gone, the drawl remained.

"You think of everything, don't you?" It was a warm compliment laced with an appreciation for his thoughtfulness.

"I try." There was a wicked glint in his eye that hinted at other things he thought about. "Shall we dig in?" He arched an eyebrow in her direction and passed her the coleslaw.

Megan filled her plate with generous portions from the array of containers. "I'll have to get going as soon as we're finished." It seemed best to warn him ahead of time. "I spent way too much time fishing. I have to get back to work."

"Oh?" Colt grinned mischievously. "As hard as it was to drag you away from the lake, I thought you would want to wet a line for one last try before we leave."

"I'd love to, but I don't dare! If I do I'll never get back to the cabin." In that respect, she had no illusions about herself. When she found something she liked, there was a tendency to go overboard. She had learned to exercise self-discipline.

The food tasted good and satisfied her appetite. She managed to clean her plate of the generous helpings she had dished, but she didn't have room for another bite.

"That was good." She sighed and set her fork on her plate.

"It hit the spot." He indicated he was also finished when he pushed his plate aside.

Megan started putting the lids on the containers and returned them to the basket. Colt lent a hand, slipping the used plates and utensils into a plastic bag he had brought along for that purpose. With everything neatly stowed away, he set the basket off the blanket, out of the way, and eased back, his hands under his head. There was a loud sigh of contentment as he closed his eyes.

It took awhile for it to register that he was settling in to stay awhile, despite what she'd said about getting back. "What are you doing? We have to go!" Guilt was making her fidgety. There was so much work waiting for her back at the cabin and all she really wanted to do was stretch out beside Colt and watch the puffy clouds bumping into each other in the azure sky.

"Take a break and give your lunch a chance to digest." He watched her with half-lidded eyes. "Do you want to end up with an ulcer?"

"I have to get back to work." The phrase was becoming repetitive, weakening as a result. "I've lost too much time already." She forced herself to insist.

"You've been living in the fast lane too long. We inhabitants of Moose Meadows nap in the sun for one half hour after every meal. That's why you'll notice we need no doctor in our community." A lazy smile slanted his mouth and his eyes were already closed. He looked so comfortable that Megan didn't have the heart to push the issue. Besides, he was making her tired just looking at him.

"You win." She decided to give up. "What's half an hour anyway." Shifting her position, she leaned back on her hands and stretched her legs out in front of her to ease the fullness of her stomach.

The heat of the afternoon sun covered them like a blanket, warming the pale golden skin of her long legs and leaving her feeling mildly enervated. The fresh outdoors air breathed sweet and pure in her lungs.

Colt had shut his eyes, and Megan took the liberty of studying him. Her glance roamed over the irregular planes and angles of his face, so suntanned and lean, and stopped to linger for a long second on the relaxed line of his mouth, clearly carved and so definitely masculine.

The sight of it was disturbing, so she shifted her glance to the even rise and fall of his chest. The thin material of his tee-shirt was clinging like a second skin; a faintly dark V showed through to outline the springing growth of chest hairs. It was no less disturbing to remember being held against that solid wall. She pulled her attention back to the strength of his handsome face, feeling that it was safer to look at the spiky lashes veiling those silvery eyes that smiled so readily and seemed to know everything.

"Well?" Colt's low tone startled her.

"I thought you were taking a nap." She looked closer at his eyes, seeing the narrow slits shielded by black lashes.

"The way you were watching me, it looked like you were hoping I'd wake up so we could leave." He smiled.

There was a relief in knowing he had misinterpreted her perusal. "I am anxious to get back, but we can take time for your nap. I wouldn't want to be accused of spoiling an age-old tradition," she taunted, a hint of a smile on her lips.

"Why don't you incorporate this little expedition into your book? Then you can chalk it up as research. That way, you can enjoy it," he suggested. It was obvious that in the short time he had known her, he had already perceived how her mind worked. It was something people who had known her for years were still striving to do, or had long since given up on.

"You know, that's not a bad idea." Her expression was thoughtful. "I don't know if I told you, but I did that with the bear incident and it turned out very well. Sure, Nick could take Sally fishing while the other two kidnappers are living it up in town." She chewed absently at a fingernail as her imagination went to work.

"Do they like each other?" Colt took Megan's hand, winding his fingers through hers.

"Who?" Involved in her story, Megan blinked at the question.

"Nick and Sally."

"Oh, yes." She grinned, reflecting on the blossoming relationship of the two main characters. "They're crazy about each other."

"In that case," Colt murmured as he sat up, "I can help you get a clear picture of the scene. I know exactly what would happen."

"You do?" Megan had trouble breathing when a hand slid around to her stomach.

"All alone in a meadow, Nick would probably take Sally into his arms . . ." With gentle pressure, he pulled her against him while his arms circled around her middle. ". . . like this."

"Probably." Megan tried to ignore the leaping of her own pulse and concentrated on what Sally's reaction would be.

Colt bent to kiss the throbbing point at the base of her throat. "And then . . ." He turned her to face him, his warm breath mingling with hers, his lips only a few inches away. ". . . he would probably kiss her."

"Probably," she breathed, held motionless by the magnetic force of his eyes while a torrent of longing was springing up inside.

"Definitely." His husky voice held no doubt.

His mouth moved onto hers as proof that it was the only thing that could happen. He brushed her lips, tasting of their sweetness, and her lips parted willingly. There were no restrictions as long as she could pretend she was Sally and give herself up to the intoxicating pleasure of the moment.

She was barely conscious of sinking down to lie across his chest. The hand at the back of her neck pulled her closer to increase the hot pressure of his mouth. There was no more need for her hands to support her weight, so they were free to explore at will, her fingers curling themselves into the thickness of his hair.

The stroking caress of his hands wandered over her, gliding smoothly across her ribs under the loose, short blouse. The sensation of his warm hand on her skin shocked her back to reality. She shifted away from him, ending the embrace. His eyes made a study of her flushed face, lingering on the swollen curve of her lips.

"And they lived happily ever after." His voice was thick and disturbed as he added the fairy tale ending.

"Actually," Megan said, laughing nervously, trying to make light of a situation that was suddenly steeped in double meaning, "I'm not so sure they do live happily ever after. Nick and Sally come from two different worlds. It would never work."

Colt rolled into a sitting position. "You mean you're writing a story with an unhappy ending?"

Unable to hold his steady look, Megan got to her feet. "I like to keep things as realistic as possible," she said tightly.

"Whatever happened to 'love conquers all'?" He stood and shook the crumbs from the blanket.

"How often have you seen it work?" A smug sort of bitterness crept into her remark.

Colt thought about it for a minute, folding the blanket into a neat square. "About as often as the people work at it," came the quietly serious reply.

Megan looked at him, but she had no rebuttal. A part of her wanted to believe, yet there was too much evidence to the contrary. In silence, she carried the blanket while Colt brought the picnic basket and they left the sunny meadow behind. It didn't take long for Colt to clean the fish they had on the stringer in the clear, cold water. Megan stowed the fishing gear in the boat and waited while he finished.

A mile down the lake they spotted a fishing boat anchored in their path. Colt pulled up alongside it. "Hello!" he called.

"Hello," the three fishermen responded.

"Catching anything?" Colt inquired.

"A couple of little ones. How about you?" they quizzed.

"Oh, can't complain. Got a ten-pounder and a four-pounder." Colt answered nonchalantly.

The eyes of the three fishermen visibly lightened, but there was no other indication that what Colt had said made any impression.

"Was that your boat we saw up at Moose Meadows?" one of them asked.

"Yep, that was us." Colt replied. "Good luck." He was already turning the throttle and moving steadily away from the three men and their boat.

"What was all that rhetoric about?" Megan asked when they were out of earshot. Water was a great carrier of sound.

"I told them what we caught without bragging and they found out where we caught them without asking," Colt informed her.

"Why beat around the bush? Why not just come right out with it?" She had a puzzled look on her face.

"Because no one likes a braggart and no one likes to tell where their fishing hole is," he stated simply.

"I can understand that." She pressed on. "But that's exactly what you both did, and you both knew you were doing it!" she said, amazed.

"That's just the way fishermen talk." Colt gave

a light shrug of his shoulders, as if that should be sufficient reason. "You'll be talking that way, too, now that you've joined the ranks," he chided her good-naturedly over the steady hum of the motor.

"Do you really think they saw our boat at Moose Meadows or were they just guessing?" She was really wondering if they could have seen them together in the meadow.

"I'm sure they saw it." He raised an eyebrow, a wry smile on his lips. She blushed slightly at this knowing look. "You can't see the meadow from the lake," he assured her, an amused glimmer in his eye.

Looking past him, she kept her eyes riveted on the wake trailing behind the boat. He always seemed to know what she was thinking. There were times when he seemed to know more about her than she did herself. It was disconcerting to say the least.

After tying up to the dock, Megan helped Colt transfer the fishing gear and picnic basket back to the plane.

"How many fish do you want to cook?" he asked.

"Just one small one will be enough. I'm not a big fish eater," she returned.

He kept out one small one as she requested and placed the others in the plane. "I'll see about having this one mounted." He gestured toward the lunker as he was loading it.

"Fine." She nodded her head in agreement.

"I'll take this one up to the cabin," he said, picking up the lone fish lying on the dock.

"You don't have to . . . if you're in a hurry," she stammered. "I mean, I can carry it." What she meant was that his nearness was still disturbing her senses and she needed to avoid physical contact with him right now.

Traces of amusement played at the corners of his mouth and glittered in his slate-gray eyes as he studied her. He seemed to be reading her like a book. "No problem. I need to check it out anyway to make sure you haven't had any uninvited visitors." He headed for the cabin.

Feeling more than a little frustrated, Megan followed.

There had been no visitors. Everything was just as she had left it. Colt wrapped the slippery fish in plastic wrap and deposited it on the refrigerator shelf.

"How about a little help?" He stood with his hands over the sink, holding the bar of soap.

"Sure." Megan poured dippers of water over his hands while he washed and rinsed.

"Thanks." He winked at her as he reached around her for the white towel to dry his hands. A roguish smile was fix d on his face. His behavior was unnerving her and he knew it.

"I have to get to work," Megan announced, her voice slightly husky. His arm flew out to stop her as she tried to push past him, curving around her waist.

He pulled her close to fit against him, his lips dangerously close to hers. She had difficulty breathing and her heart started fluttering against her ribs. "I have to work," she mumbled feebly.

"I know." He smiled, grazing kisses across her cheek and the corners of her mouth. "I'm helping you."

"No, you're not," she murmured.

"I want you to have the meadow scene with Nick and Sally clear in your mind when you write it." He feathered a kiss across her parted lips. "I'm going to refresh your memory."

"You crazy cowboy," Megan whispered against his lips as they claimed hers with commanding pressure. Her arms wound their way around his neck, her fingers burrowing into his hair, deepening the kiss. Warmth flooded her limbs as his molding hands roamed her back and spine, fitting her intimately to his hard male length. She was fused to the muscled column of his thighs. The denim material of his jeans felt rough on the tender, bare skin of her legs.

She was trembling when he finally lifted his head to trail a butterfly kiss across her closed eyelids. "It's time to go to work." Colt whispered the words, ruffling her hair with his warm breath.

"What did you say?" she spoke softly, not wanting to break the spell, but unable to believe she had heard him correctly. She opened her eyes, looking into his for an answer.

"As tempting as it is to keep you right here, you've got to go to work." Colt gave her a hard, brief kiss before he released her from the close contact with his body.

"That's my line! You're the one who's always thinking up reasons why I shouldn't work," she reminded him.

"Well, if I want my talents, as Nick, to go down in history, I'm going to have to let you get it all down on paper, aren't I?" A laughing smile was on his face as he still held her loosely, his arms encircling her waist. "Besides, you have a deadline to meet." His look was changing, becoming more serious. "And if this is important to you, it's important to me." There was no humor left in his expression. The sincerity of his words went deep inside her.

"Thank you," she whispered past the tiny catch in her voice. Standing on her tiptoes, she tenderly kissed him. Before anything more could develop, Colt was gently easing her away.

"I'd better get out of here before I change my mind." When he let her go there was a fire smoldering in his eyes.

"When are you coming back?" Megan very much wanted to know.

"I don't know. I'd better stay away a few days so you can get something done," he said dryly. "But if you need me or want anything, just fly the flag."

"I almost did the other day," she confessed. "I was down on the dock and heard a plane coming. I almost hung my white towel on the post to have you stop for a cup of coffee."

"Why didn't you?" He arched an eyebrow. "I would have loved to stop for a cup of coffee."

"Because I wasn't sure it was you. As it turned out, it wasn't. I would have felt pretty dumb flagging down a stranger to have a cup of coffee with me."

"I'm sure he would have loved it." There was the twisting movement of a wry smile. "If you just want me to stop, fly the red robe, like before. No one else should stop unless it's white."

"All right." She nodded.

"I'd better go," he said and turned towards the door.

"I'll walk you to the dock."

At the dock, she disengaged one of the anchoring ropes while Colt did the other. Before he climbed into the plane, he paused to look back, as if he were reluctant to leave. Megan felt a similar reluctance to see him go.

"Remember," he said. "If you need anything . . . even if you just want to have a cup of coffee . . ."

"I know," Megan nodded reassuringly. "If I need you, I'll fly the flags."

Chapter Seven

When Megan finished typing the page, she stood and stretched her arms above her head. That was followed by a few deep knee bends and a dozen jumping jacks. She was normally an active, sports-oriented person, but when she was writing, that, like everything else, fell by the wayside.

For three days solid, she had been working without interruption. The story was developing satisfactorily and she was pleased with the progress. The characters were believable and much more romantic than she had first intended. The bear incident and the meadow scene had been inserted, adding a touch of real-life drama and romance to the fictional adventure plot. As she read back through the pages, Megan could see a definite correlation between the events in the story and her relationship with Colt.

A vague gnawing in the pit of her stomach led her to the refrigerator. Colt had kept her generously supplied with groceries, but today nothing seemed to whet her appetite. She settled for a carton of vanilla yogurt, took a spoon from the utensil drawer and went back to the table.

The clear plastic window allowed her a glimpse of the last rays of sunset streaking reflections across the calm waters. A bird soared through the sky and disappeared. It was almost dark. Time to stir the coals in the stove and add another log to the fire to keep the night chill off and the animals at bay.

The evenings were so solitary. The night folded up the light and life of day and sang its forlorn song in the dark wilderness. Sometimes at night, Megan felt lonely or maybe a little sad, but she was never afraid. There were times in Los Angeles when she had been afraid, but not here. It was almost as if the darkness wrapped her in its cocoon and protected her until the first light of morning.

She liked this wild yet serene country. Until now, it hadn't occurred to her that she felt no homesickness for Los Angeles. True, she missed the luxuries and conveniences absent in the cabin, but not the hurried pace of city life. She hadn't thought much about home, but Megan knew that when she returned, she would think a great deal about this fresh, untamed land and the man who belonged to it.

A familiar noise intruded on the silence and her thoughts. Instinctively alert to that sound, Megan knew it was Colt. She'd heard his plane so many times she could distinguish it from the others now.

The lights skimming across the surface of the lake brought a smile to her face. She couldn't imagine what he was doing here this time of day, but it didn't matter. She wanted to see him.

The veil of night had fallen fast. Once Colt shut down the running lights of the plane, she couldn't see him anymore. Not until his dark shadow passed by the window on the way to the door. A knock followed.

"Come in," she called as she went to the door to meet him. Another knock left Megan puzzled. Colt usually knocked on his way in, half the time not even waiting for her to answer. She flung the door open, and there he stood with a large flat pizza box in his hand.

"Howdy, ma'am," he drawled with that silly crooked grin she found so irresistible. "I'm your pizza express delivery service. You did order a large sausage-and-pepperoni-with-extra-cheese, didn't you?"

"I don't think so!" She shook her head, laughing with delight.

"That's funny." He scratched his head, his face pinched in a puzzled frown. "I took the call myself. A large sausage-and-pepperoni-with-extra-cheese, to be delivered to cabin twenty-eight by the lake. This has to be the place."

"This is the place!" She was still laughing as she swung the door wider, permitting greater access for Colt and the pizza.

He set the box on the table while Megan went to fix cold soft drinks. "That pizza really smells good," she commented. "Sure beats yogurt!" She wrinkled her nose at the half-empty carton on the table. "I couldn't think of anything that sounded good." It was a shrugged explanation as she handed Colt a glass and took her place at the end of the table.

"This will be a change, anyway," he responded.

"A delicious one," she added. "How did you know that I'm a pizza addict?" she quizzed, scrutinizing him more closely.

"A lucky guess." He shrugged his shoulders. Megan didn't know why that should surprise her. He exhibited a sixth sense about practically everything. At least where she was concerned.

He pulled a wedge-shaped piece loose of the stringy cheese and placed it on a paper plate, which he handed to Megan. It was still fairly warm in spite of the lengthy trip. The spicy combination of meat, tangy tomato sauce and mellow mozzarella cheese made her mouth water.

"Umm, this is the best pizza I've ever had in my life." Or at least it seemed so.

Colt's mouth curved in a smile at her enjoyment of the surprise. "Actually, I stopped to pick up a pizza and take it home for my dinner, only I never made it home," he confided. "It was too big a pizza for one person, so I got in my plane and here I am." He took another bite to hide the mischievous quirk of his mouth. "Besides—" He stopped eating. His silvery glance scanned her features, growing dark as it locked with her green, questioning gaze. "I missed you." His voice was low.

"I missed you, too," Megan admitted, a slight huskiness in her tone.

There seemed to be little else to say. Rather than being an awkward silence, it was comfortable and natural. The portable radio on the kitchen counter provided soft background music.

Colt leaned his elbow on the table. "Did you plan to work tonight?"

"Well . . . I did . . ." Megan hesitated to tell him that she needed to work. All the trouble he'd taken and all the distance he'd traveled . . . who was she kidding? She wanted him to stay.

"Good." He started clearing the table.

"Good? You want me to work tonight?" Her hands were full of paper plates and napkins destined for the garbage, but she stopped to look at him in astonishment.

"Yep." He had an enigmatic gleam in his eye.

"You're turning into a regular slave driver," she accused dryly.

"You have a deadline, you know." It was a mildly taunting reminder.

"I know, but I can take a few hours off now and then," she stated defensively and smiled inwardly as she listened to herself. The tables had turned. At the sink, she ladled water on one hand, then the other, washing away any greasiness from the pizza.

"I wish I had a couple of hours." Coming up behind her, he circled his arms around her rib cage and waist to draw her back against him. He nuzzled kisses in her hair, finding the spot just below her ear.

"What do you mean?" There was an unsteadiness in her voice, a result of the somersaulting of her heart from the nuzzling warmth of his mouth.

"I mean"—Colt tipped his head to kiss the side of her throat, starting little tremors through her nerve ends—"I can't stay." He turned her in his arms to face him. "I have a town council meeting at eight o'clock." His lips moved to brush a kiss across her forehead.

"But it's almost six-thirty now."

"I know," he replied, trailing kisses along her cheek and tasting her lips with teasing brevity.

"But it's an hour and ten minutes back in." She imparted the information, a quiver in her voice.

"So let's quit wasting time." His lips almost touched hers as he breathed the words.

He lowered his mouth onto hers, their lips moving together in a warmly ardent greeting that would also have to be a farewell. His hands made a foray of her back and shoulders as if trying to memorize her curving softness. With pervasive insistence he kissed her lips apart, seeking and finding her open response. The completeness of his kiss unleashed a surge of longing inside her. Arching against him, she wrapped her arms around his middle, forcing their bodies closer together. The exchange lasted only a few short minutes, but its raw sweetness threatened to consume her.

An involuntary sigh trembled through her when they drew apart. Colt held her gaze for a long moment, his breath coming ragged and heavy.

"I'm going to have to leave." He sighed. His hand cupped the back of her head, his fingers tangling in the toffee-gold hair, gently guiding her head to rest on his shoulder. Her heartbeat slowed its erratic pounding under his relaxed embrace.

"You came all the way out here for just one hour?" Megan rested her cheek contentedly against his collarbone, breathing in the male scent of him, her mouth lightly tasting the saltiness of his skin.

"It was worth it." He pressed a kiss into the shiny softness of her hair, inhaling its clean, perfumed fragrance. "But I still have to go." The reluctant decision seemed to be pulled from him as he gently set her away. Then he snapped his fingers. "I almost forgot. The taxidermist phoned. He said your bear hide should be ready tomorrow."

"Oh." Megan made a face. She wasn't sure if she was ready to look at it or not. The shooting was still too recent.

"Why the face? That's a trophy to be proud of," Colt scolded.

"You're right," she concurred. "Wait till my friends see it." Her eyes twinkled at the thought.

"Right." It was a grim sound, like his expression as he turned back toward the door to leave. "I'll bring it by first chance I get."

"Colt?" The question in her voice stopped him

as he opened the door. He turned to look at her, a hardness in his face. Megan sensed it had something to do with the mention of her friends—of going home. "Thanks for coming," she offered inadequately, because she couldn't tell him what he wanted to hear.

A smile touched his lips, and he left.

For a few minutes, there was only darkness outside the cabin window, then the sound of the plane engine and running lights reflecting on the black water. The plane taxied out from the dock and was gone. The night's stillness encompassed the wilderness again. The silence roared in Megan's ears. Colt bursting in, so alive, so vital, then gone so fast. The overwhelming quiet reminded her of the night she'd spent at his house and the way the place seemed to die when he left.

The furry bearskin was draped over his shoulder as Colt ambled up the path to the cabin. Megan watched from the window until he was halfway there, then went outside to wait for him on the porch. After the way he had left the previous night, she didn't know what his attitude would be toward her now. She smiled a little uncertainly in greeting.

"Hello." He treated her to one of his white, reckless smiles as he neared the porch.

"Hello." Megan's smile relaxed into one that was more natural. Her eyes hovered over his virile features carved in bronze. It seemed much longer than a day since she'd seen him.

The porch boards creaked under his weight. "Your visitor is back, only this time I don't believe he'll be causing you any trouble."

"No," she agreed and stepped aside so he could walk past her.

Carrying the bear hide into the cabin, he spread it out on the floor in front of the potbellied stove.

"It doesn't look so big now," she noticed, remembering when it was ready to attack. She bent down to run her fingers over the fur. It was coarse, but softer than she'd expected.

Colt straightened when she did. "Been working hard?" He nodded in the direction of the fresh stack of typed papers on top of the typewriter.

"Yes, I have," she replied.

"Good, then you're entitled to a break." His glance ran warmly over her, taking in the faded, curve-hugging jeans and the gauzy, natural-colored blouse. "Have you eaten yet?"

"No," she admitted. "I was just going to fix something." She started toward the refrigerator to take a quick inventory of the choices. "What would you like?"

"Why don't we cook a couple of bear steaks?" Colt suggested.

She looked back, her gaze automatically drawn to the furry rug. "I . . . don't think I could eat one . . ." The color drained from her face just thinking about it.

A low chuckle came from his throat. "I couldn't, either. That's why I brought a pan of beef stew from Molly Louden's kitchen instead."

It took awhile for Megan to recognize the

name. "Louden," she murmured. "Pete's wife?"
It was a logical guess.

"Yeah," he confirmed. "She's a great cook."

"I'm glad." Relief was evident in her reply.
"Beef stew sounds a whole lot more appetizing
than bear steaks."

"I'll go get it." His broad-shouldered frame
filled the doorway for a second before he was
jogging down the path.

It didn't take long to reheat the contents of the
covered aluminum Dutch oven. The stew was
thick and meaty, and Molly Louden had sent
some fresh baking powder biscuits to go with it.

When they had finished and stacked the dishes
in the sink, they decided to have coffee in the
"living room." It almost felt like one with the
makeshift sofa and now the bear rug covering
the wooden floor.

"Shall we sit in front of the fireplace?" Colt
made a mocking reference to the orange flames
licking at the rectangular glass in the door of the
wood-burning stove.

"Why not?" She shrugged her agreement.

He slid the bear rug back near the sofa so they
could sit on the rug while using the doubled
mattress as a backrest. Colt tried out the arrangement first, stretching his length on the furry rug.

"Well," she prodded, "is it comfortable?"

The gray sparkle in his eyes set her pulse racing.
"Why don't you find out for yourself?" He patted
the rug next to him.

Accepting the invitation, Megan folded her legs
under her, careful to balance the hot cup of coffee

on the way down. They watched the orange flames flickering behind the tiny glass window.

"Just like in the movies," Colt murmured.

She turned to let her glance roam absently over his features. "What is?"

"A bear rug in front of the fireplace, a cup of coffee and a beautiful woman." There was a lazy gleam of contented satisfaction in his gaze as it traveled over her curves with lingering slowness. The almost physical touch of his eyes stirred up an uneasiness, an inexplicable kind of hunger.

Megan looked back at the stove. "Not quite like the movies." A slight laugh made fun of the fireplace.

"Maybe it's more like your book," it occurred to him. "Sally shot the bear, so I suppose they have a bear rug, too?"

"No. Nick has to keep a low profile. Taking a bear hide into town would draw too much attention. The best they can do is an old wool blanket." She corrected his assumption, then glanced at him provocatively. "Nick isn't in this scene."

"Good." He traced a finger along her jaw and across her lips. "Nick's on his own tonight. No more pretending—it's just you and me." The silver brilliance of his heavy-lidded gaze threw her senses into chaos.

The atmosphere was charged with an elemental tension as he moved to take the coffee cup from her hand and set it on the floor. There was a slow deliberateness in the way his hands moved to the sides of her face, his thumbs gently tipping her chin up as if forcing her to look and really see.

Megan knew that now was the time to stop. With no imaginary characters to hide behind, she would be wearing her heart on her sleeve, and she was afraid of her feelings. She knew all that. But the curling sensation inside her was the stronger force.

"Colt," she murmured in unconscious longing.

There was only a brief glimpse of the satisfied curve of his mouth before it came closer. His teeth searched out a corner of her lower lip to nibble at its softness, arousing a desire for more than this teasing and tasting. She turned her lips into his mouth, a silent moan stopping somewhere in her throat.

His kiss became roughly demanding, the consuming passion of it licking through her like heat lightning. Her lips parted under the hungry probe of his tongue and her arms wound around him, holding on while her senses were being shaken to the very core. She was remotely aware of a floating sensation, of being lifted and gently lowered to lie beside him with her head pillowed on his arm.

Her hands roamed over the flannel shirt covering his shoulders, feeling his muscles flex and ripple beneath the soft material. His mouth was on her lips, her throat, her neck, wildly delighting her wherever it touched. Arching with longing, she strained closer to the raw heat of his body, wanting her flesh to consume him.

A tightness closed around her throat when she felt his hands working at the buttons of the front of her blouse, deftly slipping them free of the stitched holes. Her body thrilled to the touch of his hands, arousing and exploring and heating her skin to add to the glow that seemed to radiate inside. It burst into a raging fire, the brightness of it blinding her to tomorrow. There was only here and now—Colt and the isolated cabin.

Hungry for his kiss, she touched a hand to the side of his face, drawing him away from the hollow of her throat where her pulse hammered a wild tempo. His mouth seared hers for a satisfying instant; then her lips felt the coolness of air. A tiny moan of protest slipped out, but it was stopped by a series of shudders that quivered through her when a hot moistness grazed the high swell of her breast.

Control was slipping away as sensation swamped her. His mouth was making a slow exploration, trailing over the slope of her breast to the taut peak. She fought off the drowning waves of pleasure with a cold splash of reality. There was a tomorrow and a next day and a next. What was happening here and now would determine her future. The choice had been made a long time ago.

Abruptly she pushed away from him, levering her hands against his chest to keep him from closing the distance. "No, Colt." It was a hoarse whisper. "Don't complicate things."

Her elbows buckled under the pressure when he leaned to drag his mouth wryly across her throat. A groan came from deep inside him. "They're already complicated."

It took every ounce of effort she possessed for

Megan to resist. She sat up, pulling the thin material of her blouse together. Her hands were shaking and they fumbled clumsily with the buttons.

"They don't have to be." She stated unevenly. "In a few days I'll be leaving. Let's keep things the way they were." There was a pleading in her voice, helpless because she knew they could never go back.

His hands slid to the front of her waist. "Things change, Megan. People change." He nuzzled the hair next to her ear. "This was inevitable. I think I've known it from the first day we met. I think you did, too."

"No." She swallowed past the lump that rose in her throat at the denial, a denial of feelings that were frightening in their intensity.

"Yes," Colt insisted thickly. "Admit it."

Megan squirmed, twisting sideways out of his hold. She couldn't think clearly when he was kissing her and touching her. "I admit that I'm sexually attracted to you." Her voice was quivering with the understated admission. Attracted was such a tame word for the raw wonder she had felt in his embrace. "But for me, that's not enough."

For a long moment, no one spoke. Megan ventured a quick glance at him. Except for a jerking muscle along the set line of his jaw, Colt was completely still. The firelight cast flickering shadows over his features and caught the look in his eyes—the look of steel, cold and hard.

"I'm not talking about casual sex, Megan."

Controlled anger deepened his voice to a low pitch that jolted along her nerve ends.

She flinched a little when his hands reached out to her, brushing along her jaw to thread through the hair behind her ear. There was a softening of his gaze as it made a poignant study of her features.

"I love you." His words were clear and firm so she could make no mistake as to their meaning.

Megan didn't know what to say. This is what she had been afraid of, what she had hoped to avoid.

"I think you love me, too." He let his hand trail down her neck and along her shoulder.

The truth in his words shouted to her senses. But Megan shook her head, refusing to hear. "That's impossible." It seemed that she had to say it to convince herself. "I told you, I can't get serious about anyone."

"Whether or not you can get serious is something you can decide. But whether or not you love me is something nature will decide." Colt took her hand, absently stroking the softness of it with his thumb. "I think it's already been decided. I can tell by the way you kiss me and the look in your eyes afterward. Am I right?" He squeezed her hand for a response.

Tears burned in her eyes and Megan closed them tightly against reality. Everything was closing in on her, all the feelings and emotions she had been warding off or pretending didn't exist.

Yes, she loved him. The strong protective instinct that had kept her from seeing it had been ripped away. There were no more blinders. And there was no sweet rush of joy to accompany the discovery, only a tearing bitterness. Why did he have to make her face it when she wasn't prepared to do anything about it.

"Yes," she whispered tightly.

"Then stay with me, Megan," Colt said quietly.

The ends of her hair brushed her shoulders as she shook her head from side to side in a faint negative movement. Colt was asking her to stay there, not offering to go where she went. It would be the same in every other aspect of their lives as well. All of the concessions would have to come from her. She didn't want to hurt him, but there seemed no other way. She couldn't lose everything she'd worked for, not now. "I can't." It was a barely audible sound, choked by unshed tears.

"Then I guess I'd better leave." There was a roughness in his voice as he rolled quickly to his feet.

Megan felt torn and helpless as she watched Colt walk out the door. It was within her power to stop him, but she was afraid to. She was afraid the price was too high.

Standing in the darkness of the cabin, she watched the running lights of the small plane disappear, and Colt with them. She wasn't conscious of the tears slipping down her cheeks, only the aching pressure in her chest. It wasn't fair. She shouldn't have to make a choice. Her hand fell on the manuscript as she leaned heavily on the table. Suddenly, even that didn't seem quite so important.

She didn't work the rest of the evening. She paced the floor. Her hurt turned into anger and resentment for the injustice of her life. The walls were closing in around her, stifling her. The room was filled with Colt—his memory, his rifle, even the bear rug was a constant reminder. The heady smell of him—his tangy cologne—seemed to linger in the air, filling her nostrils.

She had to get out of there or go mad. She made up her mind. In the morning she would fly the white flag and spend the day in town. She needed neutral surroundings so she could think. Besides, things always look better in the morning. Wasn't that how the saying went?

Morning came and with it a glorious sunny day, but Megan didn't notice. She swung the white dish towel over her shoulder and headed for the dock. After tying it to the post, she returned to the cabin and got ready for her outing. She had no way of knowing who would see the flag and stop. She was praying it wouldn't be Colt. She was too confused to see him. It seemed all they could do now was hurt each other.

She tucked the tails of a white blousy shirt into the waistband of her brown slacks and fastened the leather belt. Taking her sunglasses from her shoulder bag, she pushed them down on top of her head. She folded the short tweed blazer over one arm and closed the door behind her.

Chapter Eight

Megan leaned back against the seat with a sigh. Some of her tension was fading with the widening space between herself and the cabin. There had been a moment of panic mixed with a helpless kind of hope when she'd first heard the approaching plane, but it hadn't lasted. Almost immediately, she had recognized that it wasn't Colt.

The glare of the sun gave her the perfect excuse to let the dark glasses shield the troubled green of her eyes. Without moving her head, she sent a sidelong glance at the pilot, aware that Pete Louden kept looking her way. Megan sensed that he was trying to get enough nerve to say something, but she couldn't understand his hesitation. He had kept up a lively conversation until then, mostly one-sided—his side.

He cleared his throat. "Colt's kind of off his feed today." He announced it casually, but Megan saw the sharp glance he threw her to gauge her reaction to the new topic. So far they had talked about everything except Colt.

"Oh?" It was a carefully polite inquiry.

"This morning, when I asked if he was goin' out to see you again today, he about bit my head off." The remark was designed to draw a response, but Megan didn't choose to satisfy his curiosity.

"Are you two having a little lovers' spat?" he returned.

"What did he say?" She didn't answer the question.

"He said there wasn't nothin' goin' on between you two."

"He's right." But the admission left her feeling hollow inside. It was the way she wanted it, but she had never thought about the day when Colt wouldn't be around anymore.

"I know a lovesick cow when I see one, and Colt's got all the symptoms," Pete diagnosed. "If you want to, you can tell me to mind my own business. But if I can help patch things up between you, just let me know."

She smiled, touched by the romantic gesture from the crusty older man. She wondered if Colt knew what a good friend he had in Pete Louden. "There's really nothing to patch up," she said, attempting to reassure him. "It was nice of you to offer, though."

He feigned toughness. "I just don't want him

growlin' around the office, bitin' my head off, that's all."

Pete dropped the subject after that. Megan was relieved, because there wasn't anything she could say to change things. Thinking about it gave her a sick feeling, so she grabbed at the distraction of conversation.

"I hope you'll pass along my thanks to your wife. I really enjoyed the stew and biscuits she sent out with Colt the other night." There he was again. Colt had been so much a part of her life that every thought seemed to revolve around him.

"I'll tell her." He smiled with pride at the compliment to his wife's expertise. "The only thing Molly likes better than cookin' is watchin' somebody enjoyin' her cookin'."

When they landed at the resort, Megan automatically searched for the yellow floatplane. It wasn't there, so she assumed he must be working. It rankled a little that he was alert and capable of doing his job when she hadn't been able to concentrate on hers.

"Pete, do you know where I could rent a car for the day?" she asked.

"Where you wantin' to go?" He frowned at the question.

"I thought I'd drive into Fort Francis and do some shopping." It would be good therapy to take her mind off Colt. A new outfit always boosted her morale.

"You can take my car," Pete offered. "I won't be needin' it. And when you're through, bring it back to my house and Molly will fix you a good hot meal." His appraising look indicated he thought she needed fattening up.

She smiled wryly, remembering the diet she went on at regular intervals to keep her slim figure. "That's very generous of you, but I couldn't—"

"Yes, you can," he interrupted her. "I insist. It ain't doin' nobody any good just sittin' there." Before she could protest further, Pete Louden was reaching into his pocket. Keys jingled in his hand when he withdrew it. "You see that blue car parked over there?" He nodded toward a newish economy car parked in front of the office.

"Yes." She nodded.

"That's it. Now, when you get back, just come past the office to the first yellow house on the right. Stay right on Lake Road and you can't miss it." His arm was extended, pointing in the direction of his home. It was the opposite direction of Colt's.

The small blue car had an automatic transmission. Megan was happy about that since she had never really mastered the simultaneous working of the brake and clutch pedals. Whizzing down the highway to Fort Francis, she felt like a weight had been lifted from her shoulders. A little voice whispered that she was only running away, not solving her problems. But for today, that's what she needed.

It was still early and Megan didn't have any

difficulty finding a parking space on the main street. There were enough shops to keep her occupied for the rest of the morning. She wandered through them, trying not to think of anything more significant than the latest styles in clothing. A black crepe evening gown caught her eye and she gave into the impulse to try it on. It conjured up memories of the awards dinner—Colt, so vitally handsome in the black tux. In the end, she didn't buy it.

Around noon, she stopped at a little cafe and slid into a booth by the window. She wasn't particularly hungry, but her feet needed a rest. Waving aside the menu a waitress offered, Megan ordered coffee and toast. She hadn't had breakfast and wasn't in the mood for lunch.

Sipping her coffee, she absently stared out the cafe window. The decision she had made last night had been the logical one—the only one. She would forget. Outpost number twenty-eight, Colt Daniels, even Nick and Sally seemed like they belonged to another world. Here, in a new town amid strange faces, there was a certain ease. No involvement meant no problems. But it also meant no friends, no family, no one to care. The realization tore a sigh from her.

She was still gazing out the window when her heart stopped beating. The man just crossing the street . . . She leaned back in her seat. He only looked like Colt. He had the same build, the same dark hair and he was dressed like a cowboy. But as he drew nearer, she saw he wasn't nearly as good looking. The man held no more interest for her. Beyond him, across the street, there was a flashing neon sign. *François Beauty Salon.* It looked inviting.

Finishing her coffee and toast, she walked across the street to the salon and checked on an appointment. She was in luck. There had been a cancellation, but she would have to wait an hour. She went back to browse in the shops some more. The hour dragged by. She couldn't manage to generate any interest in shopping. It was usually one of her favorite pastimes. Today it seemed like a chore.

Treating herself to a salon shampoo and manicure was a luxury after these past weeks. Megan did enjoy that. Her sunken spirits were somewhat higher when she walked out of *François* to Pete's blue economy car.

It was almost five o'clock when she pulled into the driveway of the first yellow house on the right. It was a neat wood-frame house, nestled in the trees. Megan couldn't actually see it, but she knew the lake was at their backyard.

Approaching the white-painted front door, she pressed the button to announce her arrival.

There was a scurrying noise on the other side of the door before it swung open. Megan's gaze made a rapid descent, finally lighting on the freckled face of a three-year-old boy. Round blue eyes stared up at her from beneath a crown of carrot-colored hair. Something moved in her side vision; another tiny person crowded beside the small boy. Megan's glance darted from one to the other and back. They were identical from the freckled faces to the miniature blue jeans and bright blue running shoes.

"Hello." Megan smiled.

"Hello," they chimed, curiously studying her.

"Is your mother home?" Her questioning look encompassed both boys.

"No," they both replied, with no other explanation.

"Is this the Louden residence?" She wasn't getting anywhere with these two.

"Yes, it is." A plump woman with a friendly smile came up behind the boys. She was drying her hands on a kitchen towel. "I'm Molly Louden. Please come in, Miss Farraday." She literally pulled the two boys out of the doorway.

"Please call me Megan," she offered.

"Okay." Molly Louden shut the door and led the way into a comfortable living room. "And you can call me Molly."

The room was done in warm colors that seemed to reflect Molly's personality. The woodwork and tables gleamed richly from diligent polishing. Nothing was out of place, but there was still a lived-in, homey look. Megan sat on one end of the floral print couch. Molly chose the chair next to it, the two boys standing so close they were practically in her lap.

"And these two"—Molly paused on the introduction to give them both an affectionate hug— "are Mike and Marty. They are my daughter's boys. They are visiting me while Jana's at her art class."

"They look like pretty nice boys to spend an afternoon with." Megan aimed the statement at the two wry faces and watched the grins split twin mouths.

"They'll do." Molly tousled the tiny orange heads. Now that Megan had won their approval, they were content to go and play.

"Would you like a cup of coffee or tea while we're waiting for dinner?" Molly offered.

"Yes, coffee would be fine."

"If you don't mind having it in the kitchen, you can keep me company while I fix dinner."

"I'd love to." Megan followed the woman into the kitchen. She sat on the high stool at the bar where Molly had placed a cup of coffee for her.

"I just have to mix up these biscuits and get them ready to pop in the oven; then I'll sit down and have a cup of coffee with you," Molly said as she began setting the ingredients out on the counter next to the large mixing bowl.

"Don't worry about me," she insisted. "Let me know if I can help."

"Everything is pretty much done. The table's set." The far end of the kitchen served as the dining room. She nodded toward a table beautifully set with china and crystal. It was a far cry from the paper plates Megan was used to. "And the roast and vegetables are in the oven," Molly went on. "We'll eat as soon as Pete gets home."

"It was awfully nice of Pete to invite me for

dinner. I hope it didn't inconvenience you too much with such short notice and all."

"Oh, no . . . no." Molly reassured her with a smile. "It's no trouble to throw an extra potato in the pot."

But it would have been obvious, even to the most unobservant eye, that Molly had indeed gone to a lot of extra trouble. It was obvious, too, that she didn't mind.

"I've been meaning to have Colt bring you by for dinner before now. I know you're out at that cabin to work, so I was a little hesitant to disturb you," Molly said.

Megan tensed at the mention of Colt. Apparently Pete hadn't told his wife that they were having problems. "The stew and biscuits you sent out with him were delicious." She tried to steer the conversation in a different direction.

A door slammed and a ruckus followed in the living room.

"Sounds like Jana's back." Molly arched her eyebrows.

An attractive young woman with strawberry blond hair and round blue eyes burst into the kitchen with a bobbing redhead hanging on each arm.

"Umm, smells good," the young woman said before her glance fell on Megan. She smiled.

"Jana, I want you to meet Megan Farraday." Molly made the introductions.

"I've been wanting to meet you," Jana said. "I was going to introduce myself at the dance, but every time I started over to your table, Colt had you out on the dance floor. I never knew he liked to dance so much."

Megan smiled. She felt a light blush in her cheeks. She took an immediate liking to Jana, as she had to her parents. They were warm and friendly people. They made her feel like she'd known them all her life.

Jana poured herself a cup of coffee and slid onto the stool next to Megan. The twin boys had already made their noisy departure back to their game in the other room.

"So you wrote *The Realm?*" Jana was examining her thoughtfully.

"Yes, I did." Megan didn't know whether to admit it or not, the way Jana was studying her.

"I liked it," Jana finally said.

"Thank you." Megan was relieved.

"I've never met a writer before."

"We're not much different from artists." Megan hoped that reminding Jana of her own special talent would put her at ease.

Jana laughed. "I suppose not," she conceded.

She and Jana hit it off right from the start. In a matter of minutes they were talking and laughing like old friends. Eventually the conversation turned to Colt.

"Colt's like a big brother to me." Jana was saying. "He's practically been a part of this family as long as I can remember." The shine in her eyes showed that she adored him. It was a classic case of hero worship.

"Where are his parents?" In spite of herself,

Megan seized the opportunity to learn more about the tall, dark cowboy she had unwittingly fallen in love with.

"His mother died when he was real young—some disease, I think."

"Polio." Molly inserted the information.

"And his father died five years ago. He had a heart attack. Colt took it real hard. He and his father were best of friends. They were equal partners in the flying service." Jana's eyes saddened when she spoke of Colt's father.

"I'm sorry," Megan offered. "I guess Colt's been through a lot." She would have never guessed by looking at him. He was such a cheerful, optimistic kind of person.

"Yes, he has been through a lot. Did he happen to mention a girl from New York?" Jana gingerly raised the subject.

"He mentioned her," Megan acknowledged.

"It took him a long time to get over her. He said he'd never get hung up on a woman again. That's why we were all so surprised when he started seeing you so often. He brings your name up all the time. You must be on his mind a lot." Jana smiled knowingly.

Megan returned her smile weakly. What could she say? That she had the man of her dreams at her feet and she was going to walk away from him? No one would believe that. She found it hard to believe herself, except for when she thought about her career. It didn't seem to have the consuming importance it once had. That frightened her. Her writing, her career, had been the driving force of her life for years, her one love. Why was that changing now? Perhaps that was the problem; she didn't have just one love anymore.

The back door opened and Pete walked in.

"Is it that late already?" Jana turned on the swivel stool and glanced at the kitchen clock on the wall.

"Not even a 'Hi, Dad'?" Pete teased his daughter.

"Hi, Dad," Jana appeased him. "Bye, Dad." She hopped down from the tall stool. "I gotta run. Max will be home any minute and I haven't started the TV dinners!" She grinned at Megan.

"She's not kiddin'." Pete was talking to Megan. "Poor Max gets TV dinners or pizza every night. She sure don't take after her mother." He planted a loud kiss on Molly's cheek.

"It's not quite that bad." Jana returned dryly. "Poor Max is getting along all right." She turned to Megan. "It was really nice talking with you. Maybe we can get together again sometime."

"I'd like that," Megan replied, though she doubted that she would be seeing Jana again. In three days she would be leaving.

"Bye, Mom." Jana waved to Molly. "Thanks for watching the boys," she called over her shoulder as she went into the living room.

"Hey! I want to see my grandsons before you leave." Pete followed Jana.

The squeals of delight and then the loud rough-house playing carried back into the kitchen.

Molly shook her head. "I've got a rowdy bunch." Megan didn't miss the pride in her voice for her warm, loving family. "We can eat as soon as those biscuits are ready," Molly said.

The roast, potatoes, carrots and gravy were in their serving dishes. All that was left to do was to set them on the table. Megan did that while Molly brought the salad and dressing from the refrigerator. Jana and the boys left and Pete came back to the kitchen. The biscuits browned and it was time to eat.

When they were all three seated around the table, Pete asked the Lord's blessing over the food. Then he began passing it around.

"I thought you would invite Colt for dinner tonight, too." Molly addressed her remark to Pete.

"He had somethin' he had to do." Pete looked at Megan as he spoke. She was grateful he didn't go into their personal differences.

"I'll bet if you'd told him Megan was going to be here, he would have changed his plans." Molly smiled at Megan.

"Maybe so," Pete mumbled between mouthfuls.

Molly's dinner was delicious. When the cherry pie was offered for dessert Megan had to refuse. She couldn't eat another bite. She had a second cup of coffee and visited while Pete finished his pie.

"Megan, I suppose we'd better be gettin' you home," Pete suggested after another cup of coffee. It wasn't particularly late, but by the time Pete flew her back to the cabin and home again his evening would be gone. If they left now she could still get in four or five hours' work. She needed to after her holiday. She needed to get back into her routine. She still had a deadline to meet.

"Molly, why don't you ride along?" Pete invited.

"You two go. I'll get these dishes done up and out of the way or I'll be up until midnight," Molly said.

"I'll help you with the dishes and then we can all go," Megan offered.

"No . . . no, I wouldn't hear of it," Molly protested. "You run along and I'll take care of it."

"She just doesn't like anyone in her kitchen." Pete winked. He looked relieved when Molly refused Megan's offer. He probably didn't relish the thought of getting home at a much later hour. Molly probably knew that, too.

"I want you to take this with you." Molly handed Megan a small brown paper bag. "It's a piece of cherry pie for later." She didn't wait for Megan to ask what was in it.

"Thank you, Molly," Megan said sincerely. "Thank you for everything." She patted the older woman's hand.

The dock was bathed with security lighting and there was a light in the office window.

They parked the car and walked toward Pete's

blue and white plane, their footsteps sounding loudly on the deserted pier. The side door from the office opened and Colt stepped out. Megan's heart leaped to her throat. She hadn't expected to see him.

"Hello, Colt," Pete greeted him questioningly. "Are you working late tonight?"

"No, I was waiting for you." Colt's eyes never left Megan as he addressed Pete. "I'll take Megan home."

A shiver inched down Megan's spine. She pulled the brown tweed jacket closer around her. She didn't know if she was physically cold or if it was a case of nerves. She was conscious of the trip-hammer beat of her heart under Colt's steady gaze.

Pete looked inquiringly at Megan. "Good night," he replied, satisfied. "See ya tomorrow, Colt."

"Yeah, good night." Colt finally pulled his gaze from Megan long enough to bid his friend farewell.

Pete's car pulled away from the curb. The purr of its motor faded into the distance, leaving behind two silhouettes on the pier. The silence ran for long seconds, growing heavier.

"I stopped by your cabin this afternoon." Colt broke the barrier.

"I was in town." Her eyes feasted on him as if it had been a year since she'd seen him instead of a day. The trim black slacks he was wearing and charcoal sweater with the white oxford peeking

out of the crew neck only added to his potent
virility. His hair gleamed black in the light, his
features tanned and strong as if chiseled from
teakwood. "I wasn't home." There was a breathless quality to her voice as it spanned the wide
space separating them.

"I know." He was quietly calm.

She was frozen in place. What could she expect? Why was he here? It had all been said last
night, yet nothing had really been said at all. If
she could only make him understand. But how
could she? She didn't understand anymore herself.

"Megan," his tone was low, "we have to talk."
She was drowning in the intensity of his gaze,
swaying to its beckoning magnetism. She wanted
to touch him, to feel his strength. But there were
so many questions with no answers, so many
uncertainties.

"Yes—" Her throat was tight with emotion. He
held his hand out to her. Her feet having a mind
of their own, they carried her slowly to the
compelling force until her fingers were touching
his. Time was standing still as he leaned across the
intervening space and kissed her, tasting of the
soft curves of her lips. It was with lingering
slowness that he lifted his mouth from hers. The
briefness of it fired a longing within her. The
attraction was too strong. It couldn't be ruled by
logic.

The latent sexuality in the firm line of his mouth
fascinated her as it made its descent once again,

this time to claim hers with confidence, with a sureness of purpose. Sweeping her into his arms, he crushed her lips under his. The pressure that had been building inside her exploded in a raging torrent of passion. All the doubt and fears were lost in the whirling mist of glorious sensation. His bruising mouth was exquisite pain as hunger hardened the kiss with fierce urgency. Quaking little tremors ran through her body when the kiss ended and Colt held her tightly in his arms. She held on. She had him again, for a little while.

"We'd better go," Colt muttered thickly into her hair. "We'll get more talking done on the plane." He loosened his hold, keeping an arm possessively around her shoulder as they walked. Curving her arm behind him, she rested her hand at his waist with natural ease.

Gliding through the star-studded night, away from the scattered lights of civilization, gave Megan the sensation of being suspended in time and space. Two people alone, in love, with no external pressures to rob them of their joy, no doubts, no fears to dull their awareness of each other. A perfect blending of body and spirit in the heavens.

"Are you still with me?" Colt asked softly, his voice penetrating her imagination. She could think perfection, but reality still waited to be faced.

She smiled into the semidarkness. "I was daydreaming."

"Oh. The lady daydreams at night," Colt

teased. "That's what the day is for—the nights are reserved for better things." The dim light didn't conceal the roguish gleam in his eye.

His light remark erased the tension from the atmosphere.

"Colt Daniels, you're impossible!" Megan laughed. He always made her laugh. He was good for her. But would she be good for him? Was there enough of her to split between him and a career? That was the question that was to be answered.

"There are some that would agree with you on that point," he conceded. "I suppose Molly told you what an ornery kid I was."

"No, as a matter of fact she didn't."

"She didn't tell you how I used to steal her cookies as fast as she could bake them?" He sounded most indignant.

"No," Megan said smugly. He was trying to find out what they had talked about. She wasn't going to make it easy for him.

"She didn't even talk about me?" he said as if he had been betrayed.

"I didn't say that." Megan corrected him.

"I hope whatever she said was good. I need all the help I can get," he stated dryly.

Megan chuckled. "Don't worry. She didn't say much. Actually, I talked to Jana the most."

"Jana! Now I know I'm in trouble."

"Are you kidding? Jana idolizes you."

"We get along better since she got her pigtails cut off." He was a little self-conscious. These people were his family and it was clear he adored them. "Were she and Max over for dinner?"

"No, she had an art class and Molly was watching the boys," she informed him.

His face lit up. "What did you think of those two? Aren't they something?" he said with unmasked pride.

"They're adorable and they're so good," she praised.

"They are good boys, especially for their age. I took them fishing a couple of months ago, over at Moose Meadows. We stayed until they each caught one, which took quite some time," he added. "They were all over the trees, the bank, even up in the meadow. They had a great time." A reminiscent smile crooked his mouth. "They both fell asleep on the way home."

This was a side of Colt Megan hadn't seen before. Family and children were plainly important to him. He'd make a wonderful father.

"Do you want children?" Colt asked, with a measuring glance.

Megan was unprepared for his question. "Someday . . . I suppose everyone wants children. Little extensions of themselves—posterity." She didn't want to personalize the conversation too much.

"Extensions for posterity? I was thinking more along the lines of cuddly little tots for here and now." He had an absurdly comical expression on his face.

Megan had to laugh. "I would like to have a

boy and a girl," she confided in him. "When the time is right."

"And you want to get married—when the time is right?" He stressed the last words.

"Yes," she said, conceding the point.

"When will the time be right, Megan? Will it ever be right?" He looked at her with a sad skepticism that challenged.

"I don't know," she murmured.

Chapter Nine

The pier jutting out into the water was readily distinguishable in the luminous glow of the moon. The cabin was partially hidden by the thick stand of trees surrounding it. Megan was amazed that the place she had been so anxious to leave this morning was the same place that looked so welcoming tonight. With Colt beside her, things didn't seem so grim.

His full attention was on landing the plane in the glassy black water. By day, a pilot could easily perceive the large craggy rocks inches beneath the surface and maneuver a path between them. The night was a different game. The landing was accomplished by instinct and memory. Colt was relying heavily on both.

Megan was conscious of feeling completely secure with Colt at the controls. Part of her earlier conversation with Pete had revealed the older man's respect for Colt as a pilot. According to Pete, Colt could "fly rings around an eagle." In Megan's book that was pretty good flying.

They taxied smoothly up to the dock. While Colt secured one anchor rope, Megan fastened the other. She had done it so many times she was almost as quick as he was. He noticed her proficiency and commented on it. "Hey, you're getting pretty good at that. I just might keep you on steady." It was meant as a joke, but neither of them laughed. It only served as a reminder that she was leaving in two more days.

By the beam of the flashlight Colt brought from the plane, they picked their way along the path to the cabin. Inside, he lit the propane lantern and stoked the coals in the stove; they had nearly died out. He added a couple of logs and some scrap paper for a faster start.

Megan had the burner going under a fresh pot of coffee, while the two mugs waited by the stove. The temperature was dropping outside and it was chilly in the cabin. She rubbed her hands together in the heat being cast off from the burner. A pair of arms stole around her waist and a voice murmured in her ear. "It'll be warm in here in no time."

He was telling the truth. Her temperature was already rising as her senses reacted to his nearness. "I thought you wanted to talk," she reminded him in weak protest.

"I do," he affirmed on a long breath. "So I'd

better let you go or you'll think I'm trying to seduce you into making the right decision."

"Colt!" Megan reprimanded him, because she knew the devastating effect he had on her logical thinking.

"It isn't a bad idea." He playfully nibbled down the side of her neck.

Before she could agree with that, she twisted out of his arms. "Colt, stop it."

"Okay . . . okay." He held both his hands up in a consoling gesture, a twinkle dancing in his silver-dark eyes. "Maybe it wasn't such a good idea."

A laugh bubbled up in her throat at his mockingly rueful expression. "You crazy cowboy. I don't know what I see in you," she lied, turning her head from side to side in exasperation.

Stepping in front of her, he cupped a hand on each side of her face. "As long as you see something." He stroked her cheek with his thumb, his eyes saying everything he didn't.

Slipping her hands along his ribcage, Megan waited breathlessly as he tipped her head back to accommodate his descending mouth. He covered hers gently . . . thoroughly . . . seeking . . . probing. There was a potency of feeling in his embrace that went beyond the physical. His arms came around her, his hands moving caressingly over her, curving her to the thrust of his hips. When she finally dragged her lips from the moistness of his, she felt dazed at the depth of completeness she was experiencing in his arms. There was no mistaking this emotion that filled her until she thought she would burst. It was love, beautiful and glorious.

The smell of coffee was strong in her nostrils. It took a moment for her to pinpoint the splashing, hissing noise. "The coffee's boiling over!" She broke away from him and rushed to turn off the burner.

"We're a real disaster when we get together in the kitchen," he mocked.

"It's time for a coffee break, anyway," Megan responded with forced lightness. They needed to talk, but she wanted to avoid it. She wanted to hug this warm feeling inside her a little longer.

The coffee was poured and they each carried a steaming mug in the direction of the living room area. Megan's glance strayed to the sofa, but she shifted her course to sit at the table.

"Would you like some of Molly's cherry pie to go with your coffee?" Without waiting for an answer, she reached for her purse, which was hanging from the back of her chair.

"Do you have some?" He watched questioningly as she produced a flat, brown paper bag from her purse. "In there?" A look of incredulity crossed his features.

"I think it got squashed." Megan made a face as she tore open the bag.

"That's an understatement," he said dryly.

Tearing the paper wide exposed the flattened pastry. The gooey red filling was oozing out the sides. "It's not pie after all," she announced with a faint smile of chagrin. "It's cherry cobbler."

"Good. I love cherry cobbler." His indulgent grin humored her quick-witted improvisation.

"I'll get the silver and the good china," she continued in the light-hearted vein, wishing it never had to end. Taking paper plates and plastic utensils from their respective storage places, Megan made room for them on the cluttered table top. It was always loaded down with books and papers and she was used to eating amid the mess. When there was only one table, it took too much time to clear it for meals and then reorganize for work.

As he reached to scoop half of the flattened pie from the waxed paper Molly had wrapped it in, Colt's arm brushed against a neat pile of papers. "I'd better move these." His gaze flicked over the top sheet as he laid them on top of the typewriter. "How are good old Nick and Sally?" The pages reminded him of her subject.

"They're at the same place they were the last time you asked." Which told him very clearly that she hadn't been able to work since he'd walked out. She rushed on to credit that to a different problem. "I'm almost finished, but I can't decide how I want it to end."

"What's so hard about that?" he inserted. "They lived happily ever after."

"Together or separately?" she challenged. "It could go either way. But only one of them is the right ending for this particular story."

Colt gave her a long, searching look, reading a more personal meaning into her statement. "Since it's been following our 'encounters,' why not wait and see what happens with us and let that be your ending."

"Why not?" She sighed. "At least it would be realistic." She felt the hard probe of his eyes and bent to concentrate on her plate. "Great cobbler," she murmured, although it had lost most of its flavor.

"Terrific," he muttered and didn't sound very enthused.

Silence came and knotted bands of tension in her stomach. Megan hurried to finish her dessert so she would have an excuse to leave the table. She threw away the paper plates and poured more coffee.

Colt leaned his chair back on two legs. His eyes narrowed against the rising steam when he studied her over the rim of his cup. After long seconds, he seemed to come to a decision and lowered the chair back to all four legs.

"I've talked about everything but what I came here to talk about," he stated. "Last night, I was impatient and impulsive. I want to apologize."

"Colt . . . it . . ." She wanted to tell him it wasn't necessary, but he stopped her.

"Let me finish." There was a short pause. "I shouldn't have pushed you so fast. I know that. We should have talked it over and I should have given you time to think." His eyes were diligently searching her face.

He leaned forward in his chair, taking her hand between both of his. There was an intensity in his eyes that Megan had never seen before. It turned them black as coal and raised havoc with her heartbeat.

"Megan, I'm asking you to marry me." Emotion put a huskiness in his voice.

Megan had been holding her breath, and now it seemed stuck in her throat. His words sent a thrill racing through her, but there were too many doubts and uncertainties following closely behind. "Oh, Colt." Her eyes shimmered with tears and a mute appeal for understanding. "Please don't ask me now."

He seemed to relax slightly, as if he had been bracing himself for a blunt refusal. "I have to ask you now," he said gently. "But don't answer yet. You're leaving in two days. I'll come back for your answer then."

"Two days?" she echoed in disbelief. "How can I make a decision that will affect the rest of my life in only two days?"

"We've known each other a month." He pointed out that she was making it sound more unreasonable than it was.

"We need more time." She tried to reason calmly, but there was an underlying desperation. "Los Angeles isn't the other side of the world. We can see each other and give it more time."

"If you don't know in two days, you'll never know." It was a quiet statement, issued with deadly certainty.

It was also an ultimatum. If she didn't decide within the time limit he had set, she would lose him. It seemed to point again to the fact that any sacrifices would have to be made on her part, before and after any marriage took place. An inner agitation brought her to her feet.

"How can you say that?" she demanded, hoping he would withdraw the ultimatum.

"Because we know how we feel about each other." His response was firm and unyielding. "At least I know how I feel. And you say you do. So what else is left to find out?"

"I . . ." The truth was, she didn't know. How much of herself could she surrender and still be happy? And how much of herself could she keep and still make Colt happy? "It's so soon . . . I need time to think." She ran her fingers through her hair in a nervous gesture.

"I know. You've got to have a chance to get used to the idea. That's why I don't want your answer now," he reminded her.

When he pushed back from the table and stood up, Megan thought he was going to leave. Instead he strode purposefully toward her and let his fingers close over her upper arms in a hard grip.

"Megan." He shook her, forcing her to look at him. "Do you love me?" The question was ground out.

Of all the things she needed to think about, this wasn't one of them. "Yes." There was no hesitation, but the tears welled in her green eyes just the same. Love was supposed to be a happy emotion. Why was it hurting so much? Twisting and squeezing in her chest until it ached.

"Do you love me enough to trust me?" He still

held her arms, his grasp firm, but it had gentled at her admission.

"I do trust you," she insisted. Her head moved slowly from side to side in an expression of helplessness.

"Then trust me to make you happy." His voice was thick with tautly checked emotion.

The tears spilled over, blurring his image. Colt *and* a career was what she wanted. She suddenly realized that she didn't want one without the other. There was a panicky feeling that she was going to lose both. "I'm afraid I won't make you happy." Her voice caught as she fought for control.

"Why would you think that?" He cupped the side of her face with his hand, rubbing away a tear that trickled down her cheek.

"My writing takes so much of my time. I'm afraid I couldn't be the kind of wife you would want." They were troubled words coming from a wary heart.

"You mean you're afraid you won't be the kind of wife your mother is," he guessed accurately.

"Yes," she admitted tightly.

"Or the kind of wife Molly Louden is." He made another comparison.

"Yes." There was a little more force behind the answer because she could never be like either of those women.

Colt eyed her thoughtfully. "Jana isn't like her mother, either. But it didn't keep her and Max apart."

Her laugh was a breathless sound, dry and without humor. "And everybody refers to him as 'Poor Max.'"

"Except Max," he said quietly. "And who else matters?"

She digested that for a moment, finally glimpsing a light at the end of the tunnel. Why hadn't she seen it before? Colt was different, not like most men. Not like her stepfather and not like Pete Louden. Just as she was not like her mother or Molly.

"Look." He crouched down so his eyes were on a level with hers. "I'm asking Megan Farraday, writer, to marry me. That's who I fell in love with. Why would I want to change you?" He straightened to his full height and gazed down at her. "I know you love your work. I love to fly. And I love the wilderness. Does that mean I have to be a monk to have it? There's room for both, Megan, for both of us. You write, I'll fly, and together we'll love each other. Could anything be better than that?" A smile curved his sensual mouth. There was a twinkle of optimism in his eyes.

"I don't know what it could be." Megan smiled radiantly with misty eyes, finally at peace inside. All of her doubts and fears had truly fled. She belonged to Colt. They belonged together. Happiness spilled through her as his mouth moved onto hers. Her fingers curled themselves into the virile thickness of his hair, the blood drumming in her ears. Desire fevered her flesh with raw and wild longings as his restless hand traveled over the point of her hip and the curve of her waist, caressing and stimulating.

His hand pushed its way inside her coat, spreading across her ribs to feel and caress with roaming interest.

A pressing need swelled within her, expanding her breast in the cupping caress of his hand. Molten lava spread through her veins as his touch burned through the thin cotton barrier of her blouse.

He moved his mouth from her lips to the sensitive area of her neck. She leaned against him in a response she could never deny, never want to deny. Dragging his hand away from her breast, he shuddered in an attempt to control the desire her willingness aroused.

"You'd better bring me the right answer," he warned in a voice thickened by his disturbed state.

"I can give you my answer now," she whispered, equally disturbed and yearning to know all of him.

There was a moment of hesitation in which he seemed to be waging an inner war. "No." He loosened his hold on her. "I want to be sure that your attraction to me isn't purely physical. For your own peace of mind," he added. "I want us both to go into this marriage with our eyes wide open—no regrets."

Megan couldn't imagine ever regretting her decision to marry him. He was everything she'd ever dreamed of and so much more.

"Aren't you supposed to be working tonight?" He eyed her skeptically.

"I'd planned on it, but—"

"But nothing. You goofed off all day. You have a deadline, remember?" he teased, pointing her in the direction of the typewriter.

"I guess I don't have to worry about you keeping me from my work," Megan said dryly.

"It ought to come easier now that you know how to end it." He grinned. "As much time as I've got invested in this book of yours, I'll have to charge a commission," he said with a sly wink.

"Oh, you're a gold digger, huh?" She returned the light bantering exchange.

In one swift movement, he leaned around her and kissed the soft curves of her lips, lingering on them a moist second before withdrawing. "That's the first installment," he stated and walked to the door. "I'll see you in two days."

It was quite a while before Megan could turn her thoughts to her work. The excitement was too new, still tingling through her and spreading a glow of happiness wherever it touched. If someone had told her she would find the man of her dreams in a cabin in the wilderness, she wouldn't have believed them. The possibility of that happening was so remote, so unrealistic—it sounded like a fairy tale romance. It had happened, but who would believe it? Not many.

That sparked a thought. She pulled her outline from under a stack of papers and read through it. The last chapter was left blank. She suddenly knew the answer to the problem she'd been wrestling with. Sally had to go home and Nick had to get lost in the mainstream of society. There could be no fairy tale ending for Nick and Sally. No one would believe it.

Thrilled that she had finally decided on a conclusion to her novel, she sat down and immediately filled in a detailed ending on her outline before she lost her train of thought.

As she scribbled away, a smile curved her lips. Even her work would benefit from having Colt around.

"I'll be out at twenty-eight if you need me," Colt informed Pete Louden as he was getting ready to board the yellow plane.

"Would you mind tellin' me what's goin' on?" Pete frowned.

"What do you mean?" He donned an innocent look.

"You've been smug as a fox in a hen house." Pete made the analogy. "I know somethin's up." It was a forceful conclusion.

"Nothing's up." Colt kept up the pretense.

"You can't fool me." Pete pursued stubbornly.

"Well," Colt debated. "Don't be too surprised if you hear wedding bells before long." He lowered his voice, keeping it confidential. He'd been wanting to tell someone anyway, before he exploded. He hadn't planned to spread the good news until the two-day interim was over. But then that was just a formality. Megan would have said yes that night, if he would have let her.

"You and Megan?" Pete grinned, obviously pleased with Colt's choice.

"Keep it under your hat." Colt slid him a sideways glance as he hopped into the plane.

Initially Colt flew over outpost camp twenty-eight. Then he started to circle and come in for a landing. On his first pass over he had thought the boat was missing. He looked through his binoculars the second time over. The boat was gone and there was no sign of life around the cabin.

On instinct, he changed course and headed to Moose Meadows. It was the only place Megan would know to go if she took the boat. As he approached the open area, his hunch proved to be right. There she was, lying on a blanket, soaking up the afternoon sun of another Indian summer day.

From that altitude, it looked as though she was lying on a handkerchief-sized blanket—nude! He banked a turn and headed back, coming in a little lower, the binoculars in his hand. No, he was mistaken. She had on a yellow and blue bikini. She was lying on her stomach. There wasn't much material to see, just a lot of skin that he knew would feel like satin under his hands. When Megan spotted him and waved, a lazily satisfied grin slanted his mouth. He tipped his wings in acknowledgment and flew back to the cabin to wait for her.

Grabbing the bag of groceries from the seat next to him, Colt jumped onto the dock and secured the anchor. He had the makings of a candlelight steak dinner for two in the bag—a little surprise for Megan, to celebrate their engagement.

He left the sack of groceries on the sink drainboard and went back outside to light the grill. By the time Megan got back, the coals would be ready. As he washed and cleaned the vegetables for the salad, Colt caught himself whistling. It was a tuneless song but a happy sound.

The salad was fixed and waiting in the refrigerator. The steaks were seasoned and ready to put on the grill. For dessert, he had managed to talk Molly out of one of her famous cherry pies.

The only thing left to do was set the table. Pulling the cellophane wrapping from the red candle, Colt glanced around for a jar lid. He lit the wick and held the flame over the inverted lid, allowing the wax to drip into the center. When he had a good puddle, he blew out the flame and stood the candle up in the middle of it, holding it steady until the wax hardened.

He took the chipped china plates from the cupboard and the mismatched utensils from the drawer. They would eat from real dishes tonight, instead of the usual paper ones. He would even wash them. This was a special occasion. Pushing the manuscript pages aside, Colt laid out two place settings, with the red candle gracing the center of the table. And then he waited.

From the chair facing the window, he could watch for Megan's return. He idly picked up some of the typed pages lying near his elbow. A smile appeared as his glance skimmed over the scenes, most of which he recognized, all of which were punctuated with humor and lively dialogue. There was a sense of pride that his future wife was so talented. Thumbing through more pages, he ran across her outline. On an impulse, he turned to the last page and saw that it was completed.

A stunned expression immobilized him as he read: "Nick and Sally's worlds were too far apart. Though she loved him, she knew they could never be happy. Sally went home."

Colt felt like a hot knife had been twisted in his chest. He clenched his fists, a torrent of rage rushing through him. He wanted to destroy as he had been destroyed. Pushing to his feet, he knocked the chair over with a loud thud and forged blindly to the door. He needed some air; the pain was unbearable. He threw the door open wide, letting it hit against the wall. He didn't care that it didn't close. It didn't matter. Nothing mattered because Megan was going home.

Gulping deep breaths of fresh air, he slowly regained control of his senses. He had known there were risks when he'd decided to get involved with her. He took a chance and he lost. Heaving a deep, shaking sigh, he went back inside the cabin.

A muscle twitched in the hard set of his jaw when Colt inserted the crisp white paper into the typewriter. His features turned to stone and the laughing eyes changed to black ice as his fingers slowly picked out the message.

With dangerous calm, he methodically rolled the paper from the machine and laid it on the empty plate.

Chapter Ten

Megan tied the boat to the dock and gathered up her blanket, notepad and suntan oil. She had expected to find Colt waiting for her, but his plane wasn't there. He must have had some business to tend to. She wanted the chance to freshen up and change anyway.

Humming the tune that had been running through her head all day, she bounced up the gravel path. As she neared the porch, confusion darkened her eyes and she slowed her steps to assess the situation. Charcoals, burned white, were alive in the grill, so it was obvious that Colt had been there. She nibbled at her lower lip, wondering if he'd gone to look for her. No; if he had, he would have spotted her boat on the water.

The puzzle still unsolved, she went into the cabin. Her eyes lit up with surprised delight when she saw the table set and the long red candle in the center. Quickly scanning the room for some sign of Colt, her pleased gaze focused on the cherry pie on the counter. Warmth radiated throughout her body. She was deeply moved at the touching gesture. Blinking away the sudden mistiness in her eyes, she noticed the note on her plate. Perhaps it would explain where he'd gone.

The smile froze on her lips when she read his words:

Megan,

I'm sorry for Nick and Sally, they were a great couple. I know they could have made it, given half a chance.

Good-bye,

Colt

For a stunned moment, she stared at the note, seeing only the last line. Good-bye. Her heart sank while her mind clamored for an explanation.

Her eyes darted to the papers beside the type-writer. The outline, carelessly tossed, lay on top of the heap. She picked it up. It was the final page. "Oh, no," she groaned. But there was a certain amount of relief in knowing it was just a misunderstanding. "I've got to find him."

With lightning-swift movements, she ripped the dishtowel from its hook and raced to the dock. She tied it to fly and raced back again to the cabin to change clothes. She was praying a plane would come by soon. She pulled on a pair of blue jeans and a plaid shirt, knotting it at the waist. Taking her purse from where it hung on the peg by her bunk, she went down to the dock to wait.

There was an overwhelming guilt that she hadn't hidden the outline, even though she had no way of knowing Colt would find it and misunderstand. If she hadn't drawn so many parallels between this relationship and her fictional characters, this would never have happened. Impatiently, she searched the skies, anxious to get to him and clear this whole thing up.

Two hours later a plane answered her signal. He was an independent bush pilot. He didn't work for Colt, but he was happy to fly her in. Before they landed at Colt's office, she could see that his yellow plane was not among those lining the dock. After thanking the pilot for his assistance, Megan went directly to the office. No one was around but Harry, the elderly bald man sitting behind the desk.

"Have you seen Colt recently?" Megan asked hopefully.

He studied her over his glasses. "He was here a couple of hours ago." He grudgingly imparted the information.

"Do you know where he went?" She pressed him further.

"Nope."

"Well, do you know when he'll be back?" She stopped trying to hide her impatience.

"He didn't say."

"Thank you." Megan sighed dejectedly, wondering what to do next. "When you see him, would you give him a message?" She asked as a last resort.

"What's the message?" Harry grumped.

"Tell him that Megan said her answer is yes."

"Megan's answer is yes?" the old man mumbled. "I'll tell him." His head bent to resume his study of the papers spread in front of him.

One of Colt's pilots had a late party of fishermen to fly in, so Megan hitched a ride with him. The cabin was still and lonely with all of Colt's careful preparations as reminders. Flipping on the portable radio for company, she adjusted the dial to the local station. The reception wasn't too good, but the music helped.

Positive that Colt would come as soon as he received her message, she left the table set. There was no telling how long that might be, though, with the state of mind he must be in.

The evening dragged by. Megan refolded her clothing in the suitcase, getting ready for her early departure the next morning. She still had to fly to Los Angeles, but she was planning a swift and permanent return.

Suddenly alert, she reached over and turned up the volume on the radio. The ten o'clock newscast was on. The mention of a small aircraft and the Rainy Lake area caught her attention. Her throat muscles constricted as she tried to swallow. "It is feared Colt Daniels, owner of Daniels Wilderness Outfitters, may have been piloting the downed aircraft . . ." the newscaster continued.

"Oh, my God!" Megan breathed. An icy fear wrapped itself around her heart.

She stared, unseeing, at the radio in shocked disbelief. Crashed . . . ? Colt . . . ? It wasn't possible. Hadn't Pete said Colt could fly rings around an eagle? Tears were stinging at the backs of her eyes and panic threatened to engulf her. There had to be some mistake.

Turning the radio dial, she anxiously searched for another news report. There was a short summary at ten-fifteen but nothing to ease the apprehension she was feeling.

Visions of Colt broken and helpless, even worse, pushed their way into her mind, but they didn't hold up. Colt's strong body didn't fit the images. He was too full of life to have it taken from him. It couldn't be him.

Numb and shivering, Megan slid onto the lower bunk. Fully clothed, she pulled the covers to her neck and stared above her for hours. Sometime during the endless night of waiting, a peace stole over her. Colt hadn't gone down in that plane. The knowledge was there in every fiber of her being, although she couldn't explain how or why. Perhaps it was this consuming love she felt for him, so strong and deep that it reached out in an elemental form of communication.

As dawn was breaking, she heard the distant sound of a plane engine. She listened. As it grew louder, her hopes subsided. It wasn't Colt's plane, but it was landing.

Through the window and the gray morning light, it looked like Pete. Megan slipped on some shoes to go meet him. She didn't believe Colt was in that plane, but there was still the question of his whereabouts. He had left the cabin thinking she didn't want him. It was hard telling where he might be. Maybe Pete Louden had some news. His expression was grim when she met him on the dock.

"Have you heard anything?" She didn't bother with casual greetings.

"Did you hear about the plane?" Pete was hesitant.

"Just what the radio reported," Megan replied, her glance scanning his face for further information. "Have you heard anything yet?" Her voice was strained as she repeated the original question.

"Not yet." Pete sighed. "I'm on my way out there now. We searched until about two this mornin', but it was too hard to see." Pete's shoulders were slumped in defeat. "The longer it takes to find him, the less his chances are, if he did make it down." The words brought pain to his eyes.

"I hope you find the plane this morning, but I don't believe it's Colt's plane." Megan spoke with such conviction that she almost surprised herself.

"I'd like to believe that, too, but the odds are stacked against us." He shook his head. "Don't get your hopes up too high," he cautioned gently. "Those fishermen saw a yellow plane go down at dusk yesterday, shortly after Colt left the office. Colt hasn't radioed in and he didn't come back all night. The evidence is pretty strong." Pete's voice choked with emotion as he talked about his friend.

Logically Pete was right, but unless there was absolute proof to the contrary, she was going to believe her own intuition. She couldn't lose him now, not when she had just found him.

"I'd better get over there," he said. "I'll have the first available plane come and take you in."

"Thanks, Pete." She watched him fly away.

The dock area around the office looked strangely deserted as Colt came in for a landing. It was unusual even on a busy day for all the planes to be out. He had looked at the schedule before he'd left and this shouldn't have been a busy day. If it had been heavily booked, he wouldn't have taken the time off. But he hadn't wanted to be here when Megan left. It was better that way. She was gone by now. It was over and he could start trying to forget her. It was not going to be easy. He ached to feel her in his arms again, soft and warm against him. Unconsciously he breathed in, expecting to fill his senses with the fresh perfumed fragrance of her.

The love that hours before had been the joy of his life was now a traitorous tormentor, tearing and gouging, ripping a jagged, bleeding wound. It was physical agony to even think her name. It was too soon. He had endeavored to drown the raw pain in a pint of whiskey in some nameless motel room, but the alcohol soon wore off. Mercifully, the numbness of acceptance had finally taken over. He would make it, he just needed time to heal.

As he floated his plane up to the dock, he noticed Harry running toward him, his arms flailing, a wide smile on his usually grumpy face. He was a cantankerous old cuss, but he had a heart of gold.

"Where have you been?!" Harry demanded, his countenance returning to its customary scowl. "You scared the hell out of us!"

"What do you mean?" Colt was confused. "What's going on?" His gaze quickly traveled again to the empty pier.

"A yellow plane went down last night, about thirty miles north of Moose Meadows. They're searching for it now. We thought it was you!" Harry's words were rushed and excited.

"I'm going to see if I can help," Colt informed the elderly man beside him. He didn't waste any time. When one pilot was in trouble, they all pitched in. That explained the absence of planes along the dock.

Colt spotted the blue and white of Pete's plane when he reached the vicinity Harry had specified. "Have you seen anything yet, Pete?" he called over the radio.

"Colt! Where are you?!" Pete yelled so loud it came back static. Colt could barely distinguish his words.

"I'm right on your tail." He chuckled at his friend's surprise.

"Where have you been?" Pete asked, the tension in his voice slowly dissipating.

"I just took the night off." Colt didn't give any other explanation. It had been the worst night of his life. He just wanted to forget it. "I didn't know it would cause so much trouble," he apologized. He had a pretty good idea how worried everyone was. "Are you having any luck?"

"No, not yet," Pete answered. "I was thinkin' I might try a little farther to the east; maybe he glided farther before he hit than those fishermen thought. Them trees can fool ya."

"I'll follow you," Colt stated. They fanned out when they were in the area Pete wanted to check. Four or five passes over the region proved his suspicions to be correct. Colt was the first to spot the yellow tail section, barely visible amid the dense forest. Closer scrutiny through his binoculars disclosed a man hanging onto a piece of wreckage, waving profusely. He didn't appear to be in too bad a shape. At least he was alive, thanks to the mild weather they were having. Within minutes, a helicopter was on its way to the scene to begin rescue operations.

With nothing more they could do, Colt and Pete headed back toward the office. It was probably out of force of habit that Colt charted their course to pass over camp twenty-eight. Or maybe it was a need to be sure she was really gone. Either way, it hadn't been a conscious decision, and a wryly bitter smile twisted his mouth when he realized where he was going. There was an urge to turn back, but he fought it with grim determination. Seeing the empty cabin would be the first step in exorcising Megan's ghost.

"Holy cow!" Pete's voice crackled across the airwaves, drawing a startled frown from Colt. "It looks like laundry day down there!"

Colt's gaze jerked downward, painfully aware that he was nearly to the clearing. A muscle leapt in his jaw when he spotted the dock. Flying from the posts at dock twenty-eight was every color of the rainbow—and then some. Warily, Colt reached for the binoculars, in case his eyes deceived him. A curious sensation was inching up his spine as he raised the glasses. Did he dare hope again? His lean body went rigid as his tortured gaze swept the pier.

Megan's statement flashed through his mind and jolted through his body. "If I need you, I'll fly the flags."

The red silk robe was tied to the tallest post, whipping in the breeze like a banner. In Colt's eyes, it was a banner of love.

"I'm going down for a better look," Colt said over the radio, his throat muscles so tightly constricted he could hardly speak. He wanted Megan with everything that was in him, but he couldn't play her games anymore.

He banked the plane and soared in low, training his binoculars on the dock. When he saw her, all the doubt and anguish left him in a rush. Megan was waving her arms frantically, her toffee-gold hair blowing around her face, a beautiful, smiling face, with tears streaming down it. He pulled the nose of the plane up. "Yahoo!" he shouted as he made his turn to adjust for a landing. "I'm going to land!" Colt yelled into the mike to inform Pete. "Don't wait up!"

All he ever needed or wanted was waiting for him with open arms. Defying all the rules of caution, Colt landed his plane with reckless abandon. It was sheer luck or divine protection that glided him over the rocks.

Megan was laughing and crying at the same time. Colt was safe, he was back. She rushed into his arms. With a shout of joy, he lifted her off her feet in a bear hug, whirling her around and around, laughing with unbounded happiness.

"You crazy cowboy!" Megan sobbed, but she wrapped her arms tighter around his neck. In his arms was the only place in the world she ever wanted to be.

When he finally set her down, his mouth came down to bruise her lips in a kiss. She leaned heavily against the wide wall of his chest, wanting to absorb him. Colt pulled her back to look into her face.

"I thought Sally went home," he stated thickly as he dried the tears from her cheeks with the back of his hand.

"Sally did go home, but I'm staying." Her eyes were filled with love for him. "As you once phrased it, 'Nick and Sally are on their own.' No more pretending, it's just you and me."

"And breakfast at midnight and steaks at ten o'clock in the morning," Colt added. The perpetual twinkle was back in his eyes, but now there was an added dimension.

"You don't mind?" she asked searchingly.

"I don't mind eating steak every morning as long as it's with you," he said with sober intensity as he lightly caressed her lips with a kiss.

"The table is still set," she offered.

"That can wait," he stated firmly. The hunger they both felt couldn't be satisfied with a steak. He wrapped her tightly in his arms and the feasting began.

Genuine Silhouette sterling silver bookmark for only $15.95!

What a beautiful way to hold your place in your current romance! This genuine sterling silver bookmark, with the distinctive Silhouette symbol in elegant black, measures 1½" long and 1" wide. It makes a beautiful gift for yourself, and for every romantic you know! And, at only $15.95 each, including all postage and handling charges, you'll want to order several now, while supplies last.

Send your name and address with check or money order for $15.95 per bookmark ordered to
Simon & Schuster Enterprises
120 Brighton Rd., P.O. Box 5020
Clifton, N.J. 07012
Attn: Bookmark

Bookmarks can be ordered pre-paid only. No charges will be accepted. Please allow 4-6 weeks for delivery.

N.Y. State Residents
Please Add Sales Tax

IT'S YOUR OWN SPECIAL TIME
Contemporary romances for today's women.
Each month, six very special love stories will be yours
from SILHOUETTE.

$1.75 each

☐ 100 Stanford	☐ 128 Hampson	☐ 157 Vitek	☐ 184 Hardy
☐ 101 Hardy	☐ 129 Converse	☐ 158 Reynolds	☐ 185 Hampson
☐ 102 Hastings	☐ 130 Hardy	☐ 159 Tracy	☐ 186 Howard
☐ 103 Cork	☐ 131 Stanford	☐ 160 Hampson	☐ 187 Scott
☐ 104 Vitek	☐ 132 Wisdom	☐ 161 Trent	☐ 188 Cork
☐ 105 Eden	☐ 133 Rowe	☐ 162 Ashby	☐ 189 Stephens
☐ 106 Dailey	☐ 134 Charles	☐ 163 Roberts	☐ 190 Hampson
☐ 107 Bright	☐ 135 Logan	☐ 164 Browning	☐ 191 Browning
☐ 108 Hampson	☐ 136 Hampson	☐ 165 Young	☐ 192 John
☐ 109 Vernon	☐ 137 Hunter	☐ 166 Wisdom	☐ 193 Trent
☐ 110 Trent	☐ 138 Wilson	☐ 167 Hunter	☐ 194 Barry
☐ 111 South	☐ 139 Vitek	☐ 168 Carr	☐ 195 Dailey
☐ 112 Stanford	☐ 140 Erskine	☐ 169 Scott	☐ 196 Hampson
☐ 113 Browning	☐ 142 Browning	☐ 170 Ripy	☐ 197 Summers
☐ 114 Michaels	☐ 143 Roberts	☐ 171 Hill	☐ 198 Hunter
☐ 115 John	☐ 144 Goforth	☐ 172 Browning	☐ 199 Roberts
☐ 116 Lindley	☐ 145 Hope	☐ 173 Camp	☐ 200 Lloyd
☐ 117 Scott	☐ 146 Michaels	☐ 174 Sinclair	☐ 201 Starr
☐ 118 Dailey	☐ 147 Hampson	☐ 175 Jarrett	☐ 202 Hampson
☐ 119 Hampson	☐ 148 Cork	☐ 176 Vitek	☐ 203 Browning
☐ 120 Carroll	☐ 149 Saunders	☐ 177 Dailey	☐ 204 Carroll
☐ 121 Langan	☐ 150 Major	☐ 178 Hampson	☐ 205 Maxam
☐ 122 Scofield	☐ 151 Hampson	☐ 179 Beckman	☐ 206 Manning
☐ 123 Sinclair	☐ 152 Halston	☐ 180 Roberts	☐ 207 Windham
☐ 124 Beckman	☐ 153 Dailey	☐ 181 Terrill	
☐ 125 Bright	☐ 154 Beckman	☐ 182 Clay	
☐ 126 St. George	☐ 155 Hampson	☐ 183 Stanley	
☐ 127 Roberts	☐ 156 Sawyer		

READERS' COMMENTS ON SILHOUETTE ROMANCES:

"I would like to congratulate you on the most wonderful books I've had the pleasure of reading. They are a tremendous joy to those of us who have yet to meet the man of our dreams. From reading your books I quite truly believe that he will some-day appear before me like a prince!"

—L.L.*, Hollandale, MS

"Your books are great, wholesome fiction, always with an upbeat, happy ending. Thank you."

—M.D., Massena, NY

"My boyfriend always teases me about Silhouette Books. He asks me, how's my love life and natu-rally I say terrific, but I tell him that there is always room for a little more romance from Sil-houette."

—F.N., Ontario, Canada

"I would like to sincerely express my gratitude to you and your staff for bringing the pleasure of your publications to my attention. Your books are well written, mature and very contemporary."

—D.D., Staten Island, NY

*names available on request